A CHILD ALONE

The mother died thinking her baby was a child
of God. The father saw his deaf-and-dumb
daughter as a punishment for his own sins.
Accursed and unnamed, the child grew to her
fifteenth year in ignorance. Love for a baby
drew her into the human world. Then—
suddenly—the baby died. The broken-hearted
girl was taken in by the local priest. Working
in the dark, ancient church, the girl was lonely
and unhappy until the day she found another
child to love—a beautiful child made of marble.

A SINGLE LIGHT

by Maia Wojciechowska

A SINGLE LIGHT
BY MAIA WOJCIECHOWSKA

BANTAM BOOKS · TORONTO · NEW YORK · LONDON

This low-priced Bantam Book
has been completely reset in a type face
designed for easy reading, and was printed
from new plates. It contains the complete
text of the original hard-cover edition.
NOT ONE WORD HAS BEEN OMITTED.

RL 5, IL 7-up

A SINGLE LIGHT

A Bantam Book / published by arrangement with
Harper & Row, Publishers, Incorporated

PRINTING HISTORY
Harper & Row edition published 1968
Bantam edition / August 1971

2nd printing .... August 1971	5th printing .... January 1974
3rd printing .... July 1972	6th printing .... May 1975
4th printing .... February 1973	7th printing .. September 1976
8th printing .... October 1978	

ISBN 0-553-12613-X

Published simultaneously in the United States and Canada

Bantam Books are published by Bantam Books, Inc. Its trade-
mark, consisting of the words "Bantam Books" and the por-
trayal of a bantam, is registered in the United States Patent
Office and in other countries. Marca Registrada. Bantam
Books, Inc., 666 Fifth Avenue, New York, New York 10019.

PRINTED IN THE UNITED STATES OF AMERICA

To Galen, for being a friend,
to Oriana, for just being,
and
to Paula, because she was.

a single light

part one

the girl

Yo no sé lo que yo tengo
ni sé lo que me hace falta,
que siempre espero una cosa
que no sé como se llama.

—FERRAN

[I don't know what I have
or what I lack,
or the name of what it is
I seek.]

chapter one

Until she was fifteen she was more an animal than a human being. With an animal's instinct she searched out warmth, hid from darkness, feared hunger and cold. Had it not been for her father, she would have been known as the village idiot. But no one would call her that because he was a man of pride, and she was his daughter.

At twenty Ramón de Prada had gone to Madrid to look for his fortune. A year later he came back to wed the girl everyone knew he would marry. He came back in a stylish gray suit, a silk shirt and tie, patent leather shoes, and a soft felt hat. The fortune he had found was all in those clothes, but the villagers of Almas were impressed by it. The wedding was the most memorable event in the village since the end of the Spanish Civil

War. It was followed by five days of celebration. The bride was the most beautiful girl in all of Andalucía, or so the villagers believed, and the groom was the most envied of men.

After the wedding Ramón de Prada did not work. It would have been beneath his station in life—that of an adventurer and a traveler—to do the usual chores of a farmer. No one, not even his own father, expected that of him. Instead, he held court in his house or at the village bar. He would talk of the wonders of the capital, of the people he had seen, of the things he had experienced, and of the jobs he had had. He was a very good talker, holding his audience spellbound, knowing how to prolong suspense and how to lengthen a story without boring. Each day, every day, he would wear his city clothes, and each day the men of Almas would listen to him.

The time for planting came, and the women of the village went out alone into the fields with the seeds and the plow horses. The time of the harvest came, and the women did the work of bringing in the crops while the men still sat listening to Ramón de Prada. Later some would say that Ramón's daughter was born as she was because her mother had to work so hard before her birth, but other children born at that time were not like Ramón's child.

"Only angels don't cry," Ramón's wife said proudly of her baby. "Only angels don't make a sound when they are hungry."

The child had the mother's black eyes, but they were immense and so black that no light seemed to penetrate their darkness. Those eyes had frightened the midwife who delivered her. "She can see into the very souls of people," the midwife told the women of the village. "Only time will tell what powers the child has."

But the child had no powers. By the time she was six months old everyone but her mother knew that she had been born deaf and dumb. The mother did not know this and had anyone told her she would not have believed it. María de Prada was ill after she gave birth, and she died believing that her child was an angel. Her last words were not to her husband but to her daughter. "You are a child of God," she had said, holding the baby tightly to her breast, "and God will take care of you all your life."

When his wife died, a complete change came over Ramón de Prada. He did not go to bury her. For a whole week he sat in a chair in his house without moving, without saying anything, without eating or sleeping. He just sat and stared ahead with eyes that seemed to have gone blind, and those who saw him thought that both his life and his reason had left him. But at the end of the week Ramón de Prada got up. He took off his city clothes, put on his old ones, then rolled his new clothes into a bundle and burned them. Having done this, he went out into his father's fields. He plowed the earth without a horse, dragging the plow behind, with the ropes digging into his shoulders until blood made his shirt red. The plow made deep furrows deeper until the earth came up black as coal, until the people of the village could bear no longer to see him work so hard—each day, well into the night, silent, with his head bent so low that his chin rested on his chest.

Now there was no one to care for the child. Even if he had known the needs of a baby, the child's grandfather could not help, for he had lost an arm to pieces of shrapnel that caught him the same day his wife had been killed. The Civil War had come to the village early one morning when he was still a young man and had left the same night, claiming a few bodies and a dozen wounded. It came as it did to many villages—with the sharp sound of guns, strange silences, and abandoned cries. It came and it went, as if traveling from place to place were a part of its trade.

The baby was taken by a neighbor with a newborn child of her own. It fed from the woman's breast and it gave the woman no trouble at all. It would lie silently all day long and all night as if not wishing to make its presence known. At the age of two the child was brought back to her father's house.

"Its place is here," the woman said, and left the child standing in the doorway.

The father did not look up. The grandfather motioned the child to come closer. It did not move but stood on the threshold, the evening sun behind her making her black hair light.

"It does not talk and it does not hear," the old man said to his son, "but it is your child."

"It is my sin," the father said.

"It is still your child. Yours and María's."

"It is my sin," the father said again.

The grandfather walked to the child who stood in the doorway and reached out his only hand to her. The child looked up at him but did not move.

"It has her black eyes," the old man said. "It has its mother's eyes."

The father did not look up.

"Come here," the old man said, still holding out his hand. The child looked down at the floor. "Maybe it can only stand but does not walk yet." The old man smiled to himself. "It will tend the goats in a few years."

Ever since he had lost his right arm the old man had tended the goats but he did not farm. The old man did not like the winds that swept the sides of the hills where the goats grazed, and he did not like the summer's sun. He liked to sit by the stove when the days grew short and the air had the bite of cold. And he liked to sit in the coolness of the house during the dry heat of summer.

The child turned away from them and looked behind her, but the woman who had brought her was gone. There was just some pale dust left on the path that curved down the hillock before disappearing around the barn.

"When it is five it can tend the goats," the old man said. "Until then I will do it, but at five the child will do it for me."

And so the old man waited for the child to grow up and take over his work. The father waited for nothing at all.

The girl grew up less cared for than the farm animals, but she grew tall and strong. At five she took over tending the goats. She herded them into the hills and stayed with them as they grazed, until night fell. When she was older she milked the animals and made the cheese, while her grandfather slept longer each day and went to bed earlier each night.

Her father's life was spent out-of-doors. When his own farming was done, he would hire himself out to pick the olives that grew on the hardy trees in the worn-out Andalusian soil. Only at suppertime did the girl see her father, but he never spoke to her—as if he too were deaf and dumb.

From the very first, the girl liked being in the rocky hills where the goats always searched for, and always found, the tough grass that seemed invisible to the human eye. She would sit quietly, her arms folded in her lap, looking at the animals. As the day wore on, she would look up at the sky. The sky was hardly ever the same. What she liked best were the white clouds that resembled people, animals, or things around the house and barn. But she also did not mind when the sky was just a great expanse of blue that curved toward the earth and drowned in it as cleanly as a spoon drowns in cream. Nor did she mind the grayness of the sky, as long as she was sheltered from the rain.

Unlike her grandfather, she loved the wind, which was always there on those stark hills, unprotected by trees. It sometimes hummed, sometimes whistled, and often roared, but the girl could not hear any of that. She loved the feel of it on her face when it was gentle, and its force against her body when it was rough. Mostly she loved the wind when the weather was mild, when the sun shone into her eyes or warmed her back. The wind then was like water on her face. But she did not blame it when it grew cold, for she did not think it was the wind that made her shiver but some other thing that she did not know.

She was happy being with the animals. The goats' eyes were not like her own eyes, which she had seen reflected in the small pool behind the barn. They had square pupils, and their shape and the softness in them always made her feel glad. She would hold the kids in her arms, sometimes three at a time. Their warmth was the only living warmth she knew.

What she did not like was the darkness that came suddenly. She feared the dark outside, and she feared it inside the house when the candle was no longer burning and the light from the stove was dead. Often at night she would close her eyes tight and she would see stars, not as bright as the ones in the sky but bright enough to light up the dark. The stars behind her closed eyes had very short lives and were reborn only after she opened her eyes to the dark and closed them again. If she could she would have wished the darkness away from her life, but she did not know how.

The winters were the bad times. On very cold days she did not have to herd the goats, but she still had to leave the house and go to the barn, to draw water from the well and do many chores outside. She had only a heavy woolen sweater left from her mother, and it was not enough against the cold. Her hands would go numb, and her feet as well, and she would wait for spring as the trees and plants have to wait for it. When it came—with the earth's softening, with the gentle breeze, with the sun no longer close but much stronger—she would smile to herself and know that it would be a long time before the cold short days and long dark nights would come again.

She knew nothing of sound. The silence around her was unbroken, endless. The world without sound was a world of colors, movements, and sudden, unexpected changes. It was a world she felt but did not understand. She wondered if the flowers talked, and how, and she wondered what animals did about communicating their needs. Most of all she wondered about her father.

She would see him speak to her grandfather, but never to her. Sometimes she would see him talk to people of the village, when someone came to the house, which was not very often. But he never spoke to her as her grandfather had a habit of doing, and she hardly ever saw her father's eyes because he never looked at her directly. Sometimes she was overwhelmed by a desire to touch him, as she touched the goats. But she never dared. Instead she would touch the empty sleeve of her grandfather's coat, and the emptiness of the cloth seemed to be inside the man she knew was her father. There was nothing for her to touch; yet the desire to put her hand on him did not cease. And, as she grew older, this was what she missed most —a human being's touch.

chapter two

One day when the girl was fifteen, the neighbor who had breast-fed her as a child came to the house.

"Let your girl come and work for me," the woman said.

"She has to tend the goats," the girl's grandfather replied from his chair near the stove. He hardly ever moved now. Sitting as close to the fire as he could, he dozed away his days. Sometimes he cried out as though from some hurt or fright. Sometimes he muttered and Ramón de Prada would have to poke him to make him stop.

"My boy will tend your goats," the woman said. "I need your girl to take care of my baby while I work."

The woman looked at the girl's father, but he said nothing, as if he had not heard.

"My boy will tend your goats while she takes care of my baby," the woman said again. "Boys are of no use at home. And I must work now that my man is dead."

She looked at the girl, who was peeling potatoes by the stove. The girl had grown tall and straight and her hair reached below her waist. "What is her name?" the woman asked.

"She does not have a name," the old man said.

"I need her at my house," the woman said. "My boy will do her chores here while she stays at my house."

"Let her go," the father said.

"I can't work anymore," the grandfather said, in the plaintive voice he always used now. "If your boy does not do the work well she'll have to come back."

"He will work hard," the woman said. "I promise you he will work hard."

"Take her," the father said, "and send the boy."

"What will I call her?" the woman asked.

"What is the difference? She can not hear you anyway." The old man chuckled.

"Everyone should have a name," the woman said, as much to herself as to them.

"Call her what you wish, but take her away," the father said.

"Send the boy over," the old man added, and turned to get the warmth of the stove on the side of his missing arm.

The woman walked over to the girl and pulled at her sleeve. The girl looked up and the woman almost crossed herself. She remembered the words of the midwife. The girl's eyes seemed very strange, as if there were hidden powers inside her. But the girl was just a deaf-and-dumb girl with large eyes.

"Come," the woman said, pulling. The girl pointed to the potatoes that were still unpeeled. "My boy will finish them," the woman said and pulled again.

She let the woman lead her out of the house, down the hillock, past the barn, around the bends in the mountain road toward the village. The woman talked all the while and the girl looked at her, but she did not hear what the woman said.

"The baby came too late. I should not have had a child at my age. I am forty-five." The woman looked nearer sixty. Her face was lined, with deep furrows around the mouth and wrinkles around the eyes. Her hair was more gray than black, and it coiled like a thin snake on top of her head. Her hands were calloused on the inside and veined on the outside, with the knuckles rising high and rough. "And with him gone now, what will I do

15

with the child? The boy was born three days before you. He is almost a man, but he can do nothing around the house. You will do well with my child. It sleeps a lot and rarely cries and it drinks milk from the bottle because my breasts have gone dry."

Inside the small house, the woman's son was rocking the baby's crib. He was short and sturdy.

"Is it done?" he asked.

"It is done," his mother said. "You go now and you work hard. You will tend the goats and help in the kitchen."

"They will give me woman's work?" the boy asked. He got up and looked at the girl. "Is she still deaf and dumb?"

"What would make her change? She was born that way; she will die that way. They are waiting for you," she added.

The boy reached for the bundle that lay at his feet.

"Eat all you can," the mother said, "and work hard."

"Will they pay me anything?"

"No. But if you do well with the goats and your other chores, you can help Ramón de Prada with the harvesting. If you work hard they might give you something by Christmastime."

She suddenly felt like kissing him, but he was almost a man now and she had not hugged him for many years. This son of hers bore a frightening resemblance to his dead father. The boy will be the same as he was, she thought. In a few years, he will start smoking cigarettes and drinking wine and soon all he will ever earn will go for that. It will be the same—the same life over again. Like father, like son. The boy slammed the door. The baby wakened and began to cry.

"Look at it," the woman said. "It is so white, so small, and yet it is three months old. It just does not seem to grow."

She picked up the baby from the crib and held it out to the girl. The baby wiggled its toes and waved its arms. The girl's face lit up.

"You will take him out into the sun," the woman said, smiling at the baby. "His cheeks will get pink and he will grow. Here—hold him." The woman approached; the girl stood very still, her eyes on the child. The woman hugged the baby with one arm, and with the other hand she pointed first to the girl, then to the child. She repeated the gesture twice before the girl seemed to understand. Then she placed the child in the girl's arms.

"I will get dinner ready," the woman said and walked up to the stove. "We will have soup and bread and cheese and I will warm the milk for the child."

She busied herself with her preparations and, when she looked up a while later, the girl was just as she had left her, standing very still, the baby in her arms.

"You will be good for the child," the woman said. "I could call you María, after your mother. But that is also her name, the Mother of God, and it would not do to call a deaf-and-dumb girl after her. Anna would be better. If I had a daughter, I would call her Anna." She stirred the soup, and with her back to the girl she talked on. "What will become of you? No one will marry you. No one from here, unless your father dies and leaves you the land and the animals. You are strong, and not ugly—but your eyes are strange. Maybe someone would not mind. Maybe my boy. . . ." She thought about the farm and the goats. "What a terrible thing," she said aloud after a while, "to be born like you. Do you know anything?" She turned to the girl. "Why don't you sit down here by the stove?"

The girl stood as still as before, the baby cradled against her chest.

"Here." The woman pointed, pulling at her sleeve. "Sit down here."

The girl looked at her with tear-stained eyes.

"Why are you crying?" the woman asked. "Your face is wet and so is the baby's blanket." She guided the girl toward a chair and motioned for her to sit down.

The girl sat down, holding the baby tight, as though she were afraid something might happen to the child at the slightest motion. And while the tears rolled down her cheeks, she smiled at the baby in her arms.

chapter three

The summer of her fifteenth year was a summer of love—of wonder and happiness. Her life now was involved with another human being. She was no longer like an animal.

The woman usually left her house at dawn, to ride on a truck with other villagers to the town of Córdoba, where she worked in a canning factory. The girl and the child were still asleep. From her mattress on the floor the girl's hand, even in sleep, would be reaching toward the crib. Leaving her child with the girl did not worry the woman. "She loves my baby," she told a friend. "I know she would die herself before she let any harm come to him."

The summer sun, entering the window at a sharp angle, would awaken the girl. She would open her eyes to the whiteness of the ceiling and immediately crouch on her knees to look at the baby. She lived in constant dread of sleeping later than the child, but the baby usually slept on while the girl washed at the well, made a fire in the stove, and warmed the milk. Every few minutes she would tiptoe to the crib to look at the child, and she was always there when the child opened its eyes.

Its smallness and helplessness filled her with worried love. She moved carefully, gently, with a grace that is sometimes found in dancers or in the young in love.

The early afternoon, when she took the child into the sun, was the best time of the day. She would spread the blanket and watch the baby reach, kick its feet, and laugh in the very private way of a child. She longed to take the child back into her arms, but she would wait, weak with anticipation, for the moment when she could finally scoop up the child and hold it once more in her arms.

She quickly learned the child's habits and could foresee his needs so that the baby seldom cried. Sometimes when its small face became contorted, when its mouth opened wide in anger, the girl felt panic, but she soon found reasons for the screams she could not hear. She wanted to be able to hear it cry but, even more, she wished she could hear it laugh. The child laughed often, in his private joy or for no reason—or whenever she showed him a flower, pointed to the clouds or to a bird, or when he was fed and dry.

Sometimes the girl would take the baby into the field behind the house; sometimes she went even further, to the familiar places where her father's goats grazed. She wished she could tell the child all that she knew about the animals, about the wind and the clouds. She wanted to teach him the things she understood herself, but she was unable to do that.

Once she walked down the path to the crest of a hill from which she could see the village. Its white houses formed a crescent of red tile roofs. At its very end stood the church with its twin spires. The shadow of the church created a giant cross against the gray-green of the olive grove. Even from afar it seemed big enough for two whole villages to fit inside.

The next day the girl decided to walk all the way to Almas and go inside the church where she had never been before.

Her heart beat wildly as she tied the blanket around her waist and placed the child inside it. She held him tightly as she walked down the dusty trail. She had been to the village only once before, to fetch some rice. She had tried her best to find it in the store, while people poked her, laughed at her, and pointed to everything except the rice. She had come back without rice, and was never sent to the village again and, remembering the shame of her failure, she had not wanted to go there. But now she was going with the child, and she knew that nothing bad could possibly happen.

Almas' only street was paved with cobblestones and ran between two rows of houses, which stood without yards or gardens in front, glued to one another by grainy, white walls. The girl's bare feet made no sound, but even those who did not see her sensed her presence and began to lean out of windows and doors.

"The deaf-and-dumb one is with the child," one woman, leaning out of a window, shouted to her neighbor across the way.

"Is it her own?" the neighbor laughed.

"It's Flora García's baby," another said. "Flora got the dummy to help her and sent her son to work for Ramón de Prada."

"The dummy wouldn't even know when the child cried. Flora is mad to leave her baby with a creature like that."

"Flora García is money mad," someone else said. "She goes to Córdoba so that she can get fancy clothes like all the rest who go there."

23

"That is not so," another said. "She had to take over her husband's job just to stay alive. They never had enough land to farm and what else was she to do with no money in the house?"

People came out of their houses and out of their stores to watch the girl with the child. She lowered her head so that she would not see their eyes and held the child closer to her. She did not like the people staring at her and was surprised that she felt afraid. She had expected the child to protect her. She wanted to forget the promise to visit the church that she had made to herself and to the child. But turning back would be worse.

"What a shame," the wife of the *alcalde*, Almas' mayor, said to the storekeeper, "to have such a creature here in Almas. Her mother must have died of the shame of having given birth to such an unnatural child."

"It's as Ramón de Prada would have it," said another old woman, who went to church each morning and night. "It's God's punishment. He went to Madrid, and heaven only knows what sins he committed there."

"Ramón's sin," said a man who overheard the woman, "is his private affair. And yet I can tell you he thinks he sinned only because he did not work that year. He thinks his wife died because of that,

and he thinks that the child was born that way
because of it."

He turned away abruptly from the women. He
felt it was beneath his dignity to say what he had
already said, and he regretted it now. Women will
talk silly, he thought. The thing to do is to pay
them no mind.

"Someone ought to tell her to braid her hair,"
said another woman whose thin hair was tied, like
all the other women's hair, in a knot on top of her
head. "She is too old now to walk around like a
child."

"It's not decent to show that much leg," the
mayor's wife said primly and turned away. She had
her position to think of and didn't want to become too familiar with the others. Her husband
was always telling her not to gossip with the
women of the village.

"The dummy is almost a woman now," said a
man to his wife. "She has the body of a woman."

"Dummies never grow up to be women." His
wife laughed and pulled him inside.

The girl walked down the street where children
played, where dogs searched for food, where don-
keys waited patiently, where people talked about
her. It seemed endless. She watched her feet so
that she would not stumble or fall, and she tried
not to feel ashamed.

"Is she going to church?"

"What would she want there?"

"Maybe the child is sick?"

"Or maybe she expects a miracle?"

"She should go to Lourdes," a pious old woman said and coughed. "I should go there myself, but it is at the other side of the world. I will never get there."

"Remember when she was born," someone asked, "and the midwife's warnings about her? About the powers she might have?"

There was laughter at the memory of it now. The people laughed not because they were cruel, though cruelty was a part of them, but because they could not believe that this poor deaf-and-dumb girl should be feared. There were many inexplicable things in their lives, things over which they had no control. The good things were credited to God, but the bad and evil things were the work of the devil, or of malevolent people. Such people existed. Sometimes they were born among them, grew up with their children, and only later in life was it discovered that they possessed destructive powers. They would be chased out of the villages, like gypsies and strangers, but if they stayed they would be ostracized and always feared. But what was there to fear from a deaf-and-dumb girl?

At the local bar the men wondered what had brought the girl into the village. But they said nothing out of respect for Ramón de Prada.

As the girl walked up the church steps she forgot the people and stared in awe at the splendor in front of her. Above and alongside, the great doors were carved with statues of saints. The steps on which she walked were cold and smooth like no stone she had ever seen or felt.

She did not know, and very few of the villagers had ever heard, that seven centuries back this church had been built by townspeople working twenty years to make it more splendid than any other church in Andalucía. Almas was larger then, a town rather than a village. It nestled in a valley where poplar trees stood tall and straight, where a Duke's palace cast its large shadow from a mountain crest. The town had big houses built of wood, and two town squares. It withstood many an invasion in its day, but during the Moorish wars it was burned to the ground. The church alone remained, because it was the only structure made of stone. Through the centuries the church had been looted and robbed of its original art, of the priests' golden garments, of chalices with jewels sunk deep into precious metals. But the walls of stone remained untouched by man, corroded only slightly by time, chipped at by the weather and the winter winds on the outside. It still stood, firm on its foundation, rooted to the ground, with its twin bell-towers stabbing the low-flying clouds.

A small door had been cut into the great portal. The girl pushed it open and walked out of the bright daylight into the cool darkness of the church. As the door closed behind her, she suddenly felt a great peace settle over her. The feeling was strange, but it was a certainty—a fact, as the light of sun was a fact. For the first time in her life she had found a place that seemed to welcome her. She shivered as she moved slowly up the great nave toward the darkly-shining stone altar, and she wrapped the blanket more tightly around the sleeping baby to protect it against the coolness. The interior was of roughhewn stone, the floors of marble, and the statues looked new. The saints were dressed in robes of satin and velvet, their necks hung with beads, rosaries, and velvet ribbons with medallions rusting at their knotted ends. A large cross was suspended from the ceiling. She saw Christ's lowered head, His half-closed eyes, and the pain on His face, and she wondered who had hurt Him and why.

Her shadow moved toward the somber light of the candles shimmering inside the recesses of side altars. She did not pray because she did not know about prayers; yet she stood for a long time in front of the golden triptych and felt at peace.

chapter four

The earth lay parched and scarred with cracks. There had been no wind for days. Spring had come late and now, at the end of August, wheat was still not ready for harvesting. The animals were restless, the people exhausted from the heat caught in the trap of the valley. Over the waterless land, the birds moaned. In the evening the villagers watched the sun dissolve in the cup of the distant hills. They wanted rain yet they feared it. The guessing at whether to bring in the unready harvest or to wait played on their nerves.

One morning a white silence from the windless hills collided with the burning sun. By noontime the sky in the north darkened. And after that, disaster struck. It came with hail that bent low and broke the wheat stalks, shook the unripened olives from the trees, slew the vegetables row by row, and untwisted the vines from their dwarfed trunks. Hail beat down on the terrified animals, slashed at the people with the force of leather straps, and thundered on the housetops. By two o'clock that afternoon the sky unleashed rain.

The only person in Almas unaware of the sounds of the disaster was the girl. She was preoccupied with the child. He was not well. She had known it ever since that morning. By placing her hand on the baby's chest and on his lips, she had noticed a change. She had known it by the way he trembled in his sleep and by the way he wakened, suddenly, as if shaken by a strong arm.

He had cried out at the sound of the hail and then stopped, his eyes blank. The baby's eyes had changed; there seemed to be no light in them. By the time the mid-day darkness and the rain came, the girl had tried to feed the child several times, but each time the baby struggled away from the bottle. She rocked him in her arms, afraid to leave him in the crib, afraid to leave him alone for a second. She waited for evening to come, for the baby's mother to arrive, but the mother did not return that night.

At midnight, when the girl placed her hand on the baby's chest, its heart had ceased to beat. She held the child tightly, stroked his head and his arms, brushed his lips with hers. But the child grew cold. The girl lit the fire and sat holding the child to the warming flame. He did not move; he did not breathe against her hand; the heart was still, the body cold and terribly white. Yet she continued holding him to the fire, refusing for a long time to believe that the child had died—as she had seen newborn kids die, as she had seen dogs die.

The rains did not cease with the coming of day. When the fire stopped burning in the stove, the girl did not move to get more kindling and coal. She sat very still, her eyes as vacant as those of the child. She sat and stared at the blank wall; saw it catch the first light, saw it bathed by the sun late in the afternoon, and she was still staring ahead of her at the wall when the woman came home.

"Ayy, ayy," the woman moaned from the threshold. She did not move toward the girl holding the child. The woman stood, with her hands wrapped in her shawl raised to her mouth, making the low, mournful sound against the voices of death in her house.

Later that day the villagers came to mourn with her. The child was placed in a white pine coffin, candles were lit, the priest came and went, and the people stood around, faced with death while feeling life in themselves, both guilty about it and glad. The girl had moved into the recess behind the stove when the mother took the child from her. She was still there, pushing herself against the wall, when the people came.

"I always knew," the mother of the dead child was saying for the hundredth time. "I always knew he would die. He had death in his blood, on his forehead, in his eyes. He gained not at all; not even the sun could make him grow."

The people listened because listening made them forget about their ruined crops and the prospect of a hungry winter ahead. And they listened out of respect, for that was how they always listened to those who mourned their dead.

"When my man died I thought he was calling the child from beyond the grave, and yet the baby lived on. Each day I'd expect to see him dead. On the road coming from Córdoba in the rain, when the truck could not cross the river bed, I knew it. I knew it had finally happened. I knew it hours before I entered the house. My baby was dead! My baby was dead! Ayy, he had no chance."

They let her moan and cry. They let her talk, without interfering, without giving a word of comfort, because they knew that with the talk, the tears, and the moans, her grief would come and go. Later it would leave the woman alone.

The time for sadness was now, with the child still there, not much bigger than two outstretched hands, his face so white, his eyes dark even through the closed lids, the growth of pale hair like a light around his forehead.

It was an act of God, the people thought. The child would never have to suffer. But later, when they walked into the dark night, they thought otherwise. It could have been the girl's fault. It could be that the hail and the rain were her fault too. Maybe, as the midwife predicted, the girl had powers, after all.

"Her eyes are like eyes that see in the dark," someone said.

"She can talk and she can hear," someone else said, and shivered, "but she talks only of death into the wind and she hears it coming when she commands."

"Why did she take the child to church that day? It was two weeks ago today. Exactly two weeks ago. They do bad things every fortnight, those with the devil's powers."

"The day she came to the village was the day before the heat wave."

"I will not look at her again as long as I live."

"We should not talk about her. She might punish us; she might punish anyone who speaks ill of her."

And so the fear of the girl went with them. It spread from house to house. Children were warned against her. Prayers were said to insure protection against her. The day the child died the deaf-and-dumb girl was marked as an instrument of evil; to look at her could bring ill fortune, to talk of her might court disaster, and to laugh at her would be to defy her powers foolishly.

The girl stayed at the woman's house through the night. When they came for the small coffin in the morning, she did not follow, but remained in the house until its emptiness drove her out. She knew she could stay there no longer, even if the woman wanted her.

She walked up the path to her father's house. On both sides of her lay the destroyed crops, the smashed groves. The path itself was like a muddy riverbed. The rain had carved deep lines and engraved hills and valleys into the parched ground. The house she was returning to was not her house, and her life seemed no longer her own life. She had given that to the child, and the child was gone.

She pushed at the door of her father's house. It did not open. She pushed harder, but it did not budge. The door that was never locked, even in the darkest night, was now closed against her. She tried once more; then she gave up and turned her back on her father's house. The church will be my home, she thought, and once more she set out for the village.

Her walk through the village street was far different this time. No one leaned out of the window; nobody came to the door. People who saw her turned their heads; children, frightened by her sight, fell silent and lowered their eyes.

The village of Almas seemed like a new graveyard near a battlefield. Nature had robbed the villagers of laughter; fear had robbed them of sleep. Their crops were ruined, and even the birds' songs seemed to lament the bleakness of days to come.

The funereal scent of incense was still in the air when the girl entered the church. She inhaled it deeply. At the main altar, a hunchbacked old man was putting out the candles. The long pole with the snuffer at its end barely reached them, and the hunchback had to lift himself onto his toes. She watched him move down the altar steps, kneel, and cross himself. When he had gone she knelt and crossed herself as she had seen him do. She remained on her knees for some time, thinking of the child. Later she sat down in a pew, and soon she fell asleep.

She slept through most of the day. An hour before the evening benediction, the priest found her. He had heard the people of the village murmur about the girl's powers, and he had become worried about her. After the baby's burial, he had walked up to Ramón de Prada's house, for he had expected to find the girl there.

"She is not here," Ramón de Prada said. "I do not know and I do not care where she is."

"Do you hate your own child?" the priest asked.

"I neither love nor hate her."

"The villagers are talking against her—"

"I do not care what they say," Ramón de Prada interrupted the priest. "They mean as little to me as she does."

"Then she can come and live at the parish house," the priest said, not asking for permission, angry at the man who would deny his own flesh and blood. From the door he turned and faced Ramón de Prada once more. "She will work for her keep and she will have a room of her own and decent food. I cannot pay her, but the work will not be hard."

"If it's my permission you want, Father," Ramón de Prada said, not looking at the priest, "you have it. Keep the girl at the parish house. She is not needed here."

When the priest found the girl in his church, he shook her awake. He had thought that she might jump at the touch of his hand, but she just opened her eyes and they were not troubled. She did not shrink from him. He motioned to her and she followed him.

The priest's house stood back of the church—in its shadow most of the day. It was a large stone house with narrow corridors and high windows. The smell of freshly-baked bread was everywhere inside.

"You will be needed here," the priest said. "The least a person can ask out of life is to be needed by someone. And those who fear you will leave you alone. You are as much His child as any of us."

chapter five

Carmen, the priest's housekeeper, was combing the girl's long hair. She held the black silky strands in her fingertips and thought of her own youth. At fifteen she too had had a softness about her like the girl's. She had been full of expectations of life but now, at sixty, she had become hard, and she anticipated nothing. The girl's coming to the parish house was somewhat a blessing to her, although she had not known this when the priest first brought her there.

"That's Ramón de Prada's deaf-and-dumb girl," Carmen had said, looking at the creature who stood, as innocent as a young deer, in the kitchen doorway. "What do you want with her, Father?"

"She has come to live here. She will help you

around the house, and she will do the washing and—"

"I won't work for you, Father, if she stays," Carmen said, going back to scrubbing the kitchen sink.

"Why do you say that?" the priest asked.

"I was born without patience. I will not spend my days trying to make the deaf hear."

"She will learn fast," the priest said. "She will be of help to all of us. She'll clean the church, dust the pews, scrub the floor. Carlos will teach her."

"And who will teach her to work here, in the house?"

"You will, Carmen," the priest said, and smiled one of his rare smiles. "You'll do your best, as always."

He left the kitchen before she had a chance to bang a pan against the sink to let him know that she was angry.

But Carmen got used to the girl, who had been quick to learn her chores. The deaf girl also provided her with an audience. As she combed the girl's hair, Carmen talked of her dead son, of a past that was more alive to her than the present would ever be.

"I made a golden boy of him. Even before he was born, while he was still inside of me, I knew that he would be a poet, a keeper of other people's dreams. During the months I carried him, I knew that he would be a very special child. Don't ask about the father. He was nothing—but he did give me Manolo." The girl was watching in the mirror, and Carmen smiled at her. She listened well and she could not repeat what she did not hear. "He would have put dreams into even your head. He was handsome and tall at eighteen, with wavy black hair and eyes that burned like amber—brown as the earth, sometimes changing color, and often golden in the sun."

The woman played with the girl's hair, twisting it around her fingers and letting it spring away from her. The afternoon sun was coming through the window and it cast its autumnal light across the floor.

"We lived in Almas until he was eighteen. Then I took him to Barcelona. He had written long poems, and short ones, in a notebook which I had bound in red leather. It cost me a month's wages. In Barcelona there were publishers. In Barcelona, my boy, Manolo, would find his fame."

She began to coil the girl's hair and imprison the coils with her own pins on top of the girl's head.

"You know what he told me, my son? 'They are no good, Momma; my poems are no good at all.' 'What are you saying, my love? Your poems are

like God's birds; they fly into people's hearts.'
'Momma, you are the poet, not I,' he would say."

The woman laughed and to the girl she seemed
suddenly young. The girl loved the way her hair
was being stroked with the comb, caressed by
Carmen's hand.

"He said that to me! Imagine, calling me a
poet! And I can't even read. I'd make him recite
his poems to me and I would cry."

Carmen left some strands of the girl's hair un-
done and sat down on a chair, her hands folded in
her lap.

"In Barcelona, I went from one place to the
next—into offices with heavy doors. The office girls
looked down their noses at me. I would leave the
red leather notebook on their desks, and those
girls would say, 'Thank you, we'll let you know.' I
had a strange feeling each time that they did not
understand and would not show the notebook to
the right person. But when I came back to pick
up the notebook, there would be a note. The note
always said the same thing: 'Sorry....' And my
son would only laugh and say, 'You are the poet,
not I.'

"Oh, I asked him so many times to go to the
publishers himself! If they could only see him, they
would know what a great poet he was. But he
wouldn't do that. I bought him another note-

book, of green leather. He never opened it. He never even put his name inside. I still have it in my trunk."

She shivered. The girl moved from the mirror and sat on the floor by the woman's feet and looked up at her worriedly. She knew the woman was no longer happy, but that was all she knew.

"It was a bad winter. The winds came through the cracks in the walls and he caught a cold. There were doctor bills to be paid, and medicine. But by Christmastime he got well. One day I came back from work and found him wearing a new jacket. It was of black leather and shone like your hair. 'Where did you get it?' I asked. He didn't look at me. 'I found it,' he said. He had never lied to me before. My Manolo had never lied but he was lying now. I should have done something then, but I tried to believe that he was telling the truth.

"For Christmas he gave me a coat, with lamb's fur at the collar. I cried and did not tell him that I knew he had stolen it. He did it for me. He looked so happy when he gave it to me. He looked so proud when I went out wearing it."

There were tears in Carmen's eyes. The girl tried awkwardly to put an arm around her, but Carmen shook the girl's arm away and rubbed roughly at her cheeks. The girl moved away, afraid she had displeased the woman with her gesture. Could it be, she wondered, that only children do not shrink away from a touch? It had happened again, as it used to happen when she tried to reach her father and her grandfather; a human being had pulled away from her touch.

"I need no pity," Carmen was saying, her voice hard. "It was I who killed him as if I had plunged the knife into his heart. I had no right to make his dreams for him! Had I not bought him that red leather book, had I not told him that he was a poet, he might have stayed in Almas and lived."

She sat for a moment, very still, her eyes drying. Then she got up and motioned the girl back to her seat in front of the mirror and resumed her job of putting the girl's hair up in a knot. Her voice, when she spoke again, was monotonous, as if she were reciting a story she had often told, though she had never told it to anyone before.

"Whoever it was, they must have chased him a long time, because his shirt, red with blood, was also stained with sweat. He had been trying to reach our room on the third floor. I found him on the first landing. 'Destroy the notebook,' he said, and tried to smile. He was already dead by the time I carried him up the stairs."

The last strand of hair on the girl's head was now in place. The woman stood back and looked at the girl in the mirror, and their eyes met.

"Who can tell," Carmen said to the girl. "Maybe love can kill better than hate. All I know is that I will not take a chance at loving anyone. So don't look at me with begging eyes. I have nothing to give to you or to anyone."

She went out and shut the door behind her, and with the closing of the door she shut the girl out of her life. It was done. The past now had words. There was no bond between her and the deaf-and-dumb girl. She could not take her for a daughter because she was afraid to see love turn to death again.

For a long time the girl sat in front of the mirror, looking down at her folded arms. She was thinking of Carmen, remembering the changes on her face, trying to guess what had caused her tears and made her leave the room so suddenly. When she finally looked at her own reflection, she saw a face streaked with tears—a stranger's face.

Her cheekbones seemed to have grown high and sharp, her eyes very large, with a shiny blackness in them. Her hair, brushed very smoothly up from her neck and away from her temples, ended in a knot on top of her head, not unlike the knot all the women of the village wore. I look like the others, the girl thought.

But she knew that she was not like them.

chapter six

The girl saw that the priest was not a happy man. He hardly ever smiled. He never laughed. His thin face looked tortured, and each day the line between his brows grew deeper, the circles under his eyes darker. Often when the girl served his meals, he would be so lost in thought that the food on his plate went untouched, the glass of wine suspended in his hand.

The priest was an austere and a solitary man. Masses, confessions, deaths, marriages, baptisms, and sicknesses—each with their different demands—occupied his time. But his days were long, and his works did not relieve him from an ever-present sense of his own worthlessness. The needs he fulfilled were not enough, he felt, to justify his life. He was a man of God, yet he had not achieved the sanctity he had hoped for when he first thought of becoming a priest. On the contrary, it seemed to him that with time he grew farther away from accomplishing the task of saving his own soul. He prayed for himself more than he prayed for others and that, in itself, was proof enough of his failure. The more he worried, the more guilt he felt. Too often now he longed for the days of his childhood and youth, when the simplicity of his faith and his love of God threw no shadows across his soul.

In his youth, everything had seemed so simple. He had thought the world perpetually in a state of war, divided into two camps—the white army of virtue and the black army of sin. And he had delighted in staging battles between these two forces. Books were his generals then. His books did their job well; the white army never failed to triumph. But since coming to the desolate village of Almas the ideas in those books seemed to have deserted him. The banner of faith was not enough anymore; the two sides were no longer clear. Those of his parish who sinned did not lack faith; yet for them the boundaries between black and white were being destroyed by the complexities of daily life.

The priest spent his most agonizing hours in

the confessional. Each sin carried with it an excuse.

"Father, I have sinned," a voice would say into the velvet darkness. "I wished my unborn child dead. But, Father, I am only thirty-two and a mother of ten. How can I cope with another?"

And the woman's sin would point a sword at the priest's heart.

"You must pray, my child."

But he could not vanquish the sin by saying that. She would pray, but the sin would still be there.

"I have raised my hand against God, Father," another voice would say. "I cursed my fate."

"The Lord taught us to love," the priest would reply. "We must love and hope for the everlasting life, not for happiness in this life."

But his words seemed like stray bullets, never finding their marks. The priest often thought that perhaps he was not concerned enough for the sinners, but only with what was right and what was wrong.

The hunchback, who worked in the church, never worried about his soul. His occasions to sin were few, and he had ample time for prayer. But his prayers were always concretely-phrased requests. He had become familiar with the saints during his long years at the parish. He would alternate his requests, circling the church from left to right, starting with Archangel Gabriel at the church door and going around until he reached Saint Anne in the nave on the other side. From time to time, with the cunning that was a part of him, he would appeal to a little-known and less-remembered saint:

"I pray today," he would mutter as he went about his chores, "to an Italian saint. God only knows how many of those there are! I don't even know your name. How would I? You've been forgotten by everyone. In the last two hundred years no one has prayed to you, so you certainly have time to listen to an old hunchback. All I ask of you is that you make my pains go away. I do not expect miracles—just a good night once in a while. The pain is worst right between the shoulder blades. Actually, to tell the truth, there is but one shoulder blade; the other side has the growth.

"It might be a long time before anyone remembers you enough to pray to you, so do your best, because God might think that you are useless there, sitting in Heaven, among all those Italian saints, having nothing to do. And He certainly would know if you helped me. I, myself, will tell Him so."

The hunchback was not unhappy, but he

wanted everyone to think that he was. Now, with
the deaf-and-dumb girl around, he wanted to
make her believe the worst. He would twist his
mouth so that he looked in perpetual pain, and he
moaned whenever she was around, although he
knew she could not hear him. He even improved on
his grotesque walk to make it seem agonizing. He
would drag his feet in small semicircles, putting
them down slowly, as though his infirmity had to
be exercised with great precision.

His ruse worked, and from the very first day the
girl took over most of his chores. He now only lit
and put out the candles, prepared for Mass,
cleaned the altar, and rang the church bells.

The ringing of the bells he would not assign to
anyone. Years ago, a passing stranger had told him
the story of the hunchback of Notre Dame. "He
was a bell-ringer, like you," the stranger had said.
"If anyone were to make a new motion picture of
the book, you would be perfect in the part. It
would make you famous."

The hunchback of Almas did not expect to become a movie star, but he liked to think of the
possibility of fame. At the village bar, where he
went every day at sundown for his *copita* of *man-
zanilla*, he would often speak of what the stranger
had told him. And his long, wolf-like face would
break into a broad smile.

The girl's days were divided equally: she worked in the house during the morning hours and in the church during the afternoons. She was indoors all the time, and she missed the feel of the wind and the sun. Darkness was now a part of her life—not only the darkness of the house and the church, but a darkness inside her heart. She sensed, but did not know, that the darkness there was caused by the absence of love, for she had not felt happiness since the death of the child.

She lived with a strange feeling of anticipation. It seemed to her that her life had been suspended. She had no idea of what she was waiting for. But when the feeling was strongest, on bleak mornings, or during the night, she thought it had to do with the child. At such times, she made herself believe that the child was not really dead, that it had all been a bad dream and that soon, when she awakened, she would be holding the child again, seeing him laugh, watching him play in the sunlight. She would smile then, and the waiting and the darkness would go away.

Although she preferred working in the church to working inside the house, the church had not become a home. It was too large. She belonged in it more than it belonged to her. The girl could lay no claims to friendship with the statues of the saints, but she became familiar with them. They had to be dusted, sometimes even washed. She gave them names because she did not know what they were called, and she invented brave deeds, good works, and even tragic deaths for them. Each statue had its special needs. The mother holding the child had to have white flowers; the carpenter needed at least one candle burning in front of his dark, bearded face; the lady with the long stream of roses descending from her small hands to her black-shod feet liked cleanliness; the priest with the silver cross held high disliked his dark corner and wanted more light; the large angel wanted to fly. Only the hanging Man, whom she could not reach with her duster, seemed not to need anything at all.

The church that she knew was an empty church. She was never there when people came; she never saw it blazing with lights. She had never heard it come alive with the voices of the singing Sunday crowd, so to her it was a place of sorrow, darkness, and loneliness. She had hoped at first that the statues of the saints would become as real as people, that touching them would bring them to life. But they remained lifeless, and she knew that she attended only to their imaginary, not their real, needs.

During her third week at the parish house the miracle happened. She was on her knees scrubbing behind the altar, when a wooden panel gave way and fell to the floor. The multicolored light from the round stained-glass window above her fell on something white inside the exposed hole. She reached in and her fingers felt marble, smooth and cold. She put her face down on the floor and tried to see what the whiteness might be, but it receded into shadow and she could not make out what it was. She reached inside again and pulled gently. The first thing she saw was a small, extended marble hand, and then a Child's carven head. Her hand trembled and her heart beat wildly as she lifted the small figure from its hiding place.

The marble Baby was no bigger than the baby she had taken care of and loved. It fitted into her arms exactly as that other child had, and the smile on its face was like that of the other child.

She sat holding the statue for a long time. No one would be able to see her unless they walked behind the great altar and no one ever did except to clean, and now that was her job. The marble Baby would be known to no one; it would belong only to her. She had found it and she alone would keep it. Tenderly she returned it to its hiding place.

All day long now she thought about her secret.

A Single Light

In her mind she would weave imaginary blankets for it; she would make satin clothes for it, and she would imagine the Child reaching out to the sunlight and laughing at the birds and at clouds. When she was away from the Child she pretended it was waiting for her, and even though she pretended, her love for the Baby grew and became real.

Each day was long on morning and short of afternoon, for it was not until two or three o'clock that she could go behind the altar and spend some time with the one thing she now owned in this world. And the ownership filled her with great pride.

The strange, uneasy feeling of waiting for something unknown changed to a bright anticipation of what she knew would be awaiting her in the afternoon—her reunion with the marble Child. Its existence was the one happy fact of her life, and that fact drove the darkness completely from her heart.

part two

---

the statue

Las cosas son como son
hasta que dejan de serlo.

—CANCIONERILLO DEL DUENDE

[Things are the way they are,
and then they are that way no longer.]

chapter seven

Although the dust jackets of his two books proclaimed him to be an "art expert," Larry Katchen was not quite that; he was an expert only on the Renaissance sculptor Angellini. When his first book was published, Larry was thirty. It was entitled simply *Angellini*. Ten years later his second book appeared; it was called *Angellini's Lost Child*. Both books had a modest sale, but each highly pleased the author. Larry Katchen had only one interest in life, and he had managed to keep his existence focused on that interest. He was a happy man.

Even as a child Larry tended to be single-minded and obstinate. His parents were easygoing; Larry was organized. He was fussy about his possessions; he wanted all his clothes to be of the same color and his meals to be exactly on time; and he disliked books that told a story rather than recounted facts. He was as easy to live with as an alarm clock set to ring at regular intervals. Mr. and Mrs. Katchen searched for quite a while before they found a boarding school with a kindergarten that would accept little Larry as a pupil.

Until he was thirteen, Larry's primary interest was spelling, and his favorite pastime was finding typographical errors in *The New York Times*. At thirteen he outgrew what had by then become an obsession and began to study insects with the determination of an ant. By the time he went to college, to major in biology, his parents were reconciled to the fact that their only son had always been, and always would be, a bore.

They sent him to Europe in the summer of his nineteenth year. "Since I only have three months," Larry told them, "I shall only go to Italy. It is possible that I will be able to see no more than Rome, but I certainly will try to give Florence a chance."

As his parents waved good-bye to Larry who stood at the ship's rail, a light woolen scarf around his throat against the early summer breeze, they both breathed a sigh of relief.

"There will be a whole ocean between Larry and

us," said Mrs. Katchen, waving and smiling up to her son.

"We should write him about staying on," said Mr. Katchen. "Being in Europe for a few years might do him good."

"My life began," Larry Katchen wrote in the introduction to his first book, "the summer of my nineteenth year, when I made my first trip to Italy."

In Rome Larry dutifully followed a guidebook. The book told all points of interest in their most practical order, saving steps and time. According to Larry's guidebook, one could not go through the Forum in less than five days, and Larry did not cut the time nor dally when the five days were up. His head assumed the motion of a man watching a vertical tennis match—down to the book, up to look at the object described. His principal purpose was not pleasure but education, and he achieved all he set out to do. A mind feebler than Larry's would have reeled under the impact of so many facts, but his was a retentive and a strong mind.

On the twenty-first day of Larry's stay in Rome, however, the order of his daily life was interrupted, with the suddenness of a rifle shot. On that day he found himself in a private gallery, which the guidebook described as "an absolute must for anyone seriously interested in that neglected Renaissance genius, the sculptor Angellini. Here one can see his least-known and earliest work."

At the door of the gallery an elderly maid took Larry Katchen's hat and the price of admission; then disappeared down a dark corridor. He wandered aimlessly through rooms that contained an overabundance of stuffed chairs, gilded mirrors, figurines, and family portraits until he came upon several elderly ladies having tea. They seemed very surprised to see him, and directed him to a courtyard where he found Angellini's statue.

It stood twenty feet high, towering over a cluster of trees. It was made of marble and represented a wounded warrior. His sword hung limply from his right hand, his left exploring the wound in his thigh. The face was ridged with taut muscles, the pain an arrested scream behind his lips. His body seemed both straight and bent, as if the agony of the wound were very fresh and had not yet reached into the marrow of his bones.

First Larry read the five pages devoted to this work; then he looked from the book to the statue and found himself deeply moved. He walked around it several times, touching it once or twice. When he opened the book again it was to search out feverishly more facts about the sculptor and his work. Angellini's true masterpiece, he discovered, was to be found at the Vatican Gallery. Larry did not wait for the tour of the Vatican, planned three days hence according to his guidebook, but took a cab to the Vatican that afternoon.

"The Holy Family with Child" was the title given to Angellini's most important work. Larry noticed immediately that the group was incomplete. The Child was missing. The footnote in the guidebook informed him that, at some time in the fifteenth century, the Child had been stolen or destroyed. Larry spent the rest of the afternoon and all the following day trying to locate more information about the missing figure. Neither the people he talked with nor the books he looked through were able to furnish further information.

That week Larry wrote his parents:

Dear Mother and Dad,
  I would like to ask your permission to remain in Italy for a whole year. I have become very interested in the sculptor Angellini. I would like to find out all I can about him, especially about a figure missing from his masterpiece.

While Mrs. Katchen read the rest of the letter aloud, her husband was opening a magnum of champagne to celebrate their son's decision.

Larry's research now consumed all of his time. He was no longer interested in exploring Rome and its art treasures. He had become completely immersed in learning all he could about Angellini. In Angellini's lifetime, which had spanned sixty-eight years, he had completed only twelve sculptures. This fact alone impressed Larry tremendously, for he believed in perfection of accomplishment. And soon he realized that he would be happy spending his own lifetime exclusively in the study of Angellini's works and in solving the mystery of the missing Child. He was certain that, in time, he would be ready to form a theory as to what had happened to the missing figure.

Twenty-one years later Larry Katchen was indeed ready to advance such a theory in his book, *Angellini's Lost Child*. From what he had learned in all those years it seemed obvious to him that the Child must be somewhere in Spain. He felt certain that it had been stolen by a Spaniard, most probably a soldier, during the Italian-Spanish wars. If it had not been destroyed, it was hidden somewhere, Larry believed, most probably in a church or a cemetery. He ended the book with this sentence: "I shall devote the rest of my life to the search for the Child."

He was given several private grants to help him

in his endeavor, and after his parents died, he used his inheritance to continue his search, which he had estimated would take at least ten years if he were to cover all of Spain.

At fifty-two Larry Katchen had lost none of his earlier determination, although his hair had turned white, his eyes seemed tired behind the thick lenses of his glasses, and his hands shook each time he approached a new church or a cemetery. He traveled through Spain in a car that had suffered much from the rough back roads. His English tweeds were badly worn at the elbows and knees and often now, to save money, Larry skipped a meal or slept inside his car.

Obsessed with his mission, he had no time for people and no commitments to them—no friendships. He had freed himself of all the obligations that life entails. Only God knew that Larry Katchen's search for Angellini's Child was his excuse for not facing up to life, to its difficulties, its disappointments, and consequently to its joys and rewards.

It was during his seventh year of traveling across Spain that Larry arrived, one autumn day, in the village of Almas.

chapter eight

The road leading to Almas did not invite travelers. It turned off sharply from the highway that linked Grenada with Córdoba. There was no sign at the turn. It was not a paved road, but rather a mountain pass that, since the summer storm, was eroded with almost impassable gullies. It climbed sharply along the desolate hillsides and dropped dangerously into the valleys where trees were few and rocks numerous. The more adventurous and curious who did make the turn, seeing no houses and no signs of life, would go back to the highway at the first possible turn.

And yet life was present in this forlorn landscape. Rabbits scooted among the rocks; lizards hugged the ground; ants won and lost whole empires. A frightened deer would sometimes stray over soil that contained every hue of brown, yellow, and gray dust. There were also patches of cultivated land where, year after year, generation after generation, men had pitted themselves against rocks and soil erosion. And on those patches grew wheat, olives, grapes, and vegetables; and they were tended with great care and love and prayed over at night.

There were also houses, invisible from the road, hidden in curving earth, or flung high on peaks often covered by fog and clouds. People in that part of Andalucía either lived back-to-back in villages, small towns, and cities or were inclined to isolate themselves. Whether out of a simple desire for solitude, or to preserve an ancestral squatting right, or simply to challenge nature, these family hermitages stood alone, on seemingly inaccessible bits of land, and only low-flying planes or birds could make out their red tile roofs, the bony dogs lying in the meager shade of a house, or white wash waving in the wind like flags of surrender.

By the time Larry Katchen's car stopped in front of the inn, the children of Almas had made a dozen guesses about its occupant.

"He's a government man."

"Stupid! Government men ride in shiny black cars!"

"He could be a small government man! Or the cousin of a government man."

"He's a circus man! Maybe even a magician!"

"Can't you see he's a foreigner? English—or maybe even American."

"No! He's only a salesman. I saw a salesman once who looked like that. His car was even worse than this one."

"He's not a salesman!"

"Yes, he is!"

The children's parents were no less curious, and they took as many guesses and had as many arguments. Some of the men got dressed in their shiny black suits and strolled nonchalantly toward the bar as if it were their habit to do that so early on a Saturday morning. The women leaned out of windows or came out-of-doors, hugging their black sweaters to them in the early morning wind. They called to one another and wondered aloud about the stranger.

"His suitcase is made of an animal's hide."

"Must be a rich man."

"Certainly not a millionaire! Just look at that car. It's older than he is!"

"But not as old as that suit he's wearing."

Larry Katchen had spent an uncomfortable night inside his car. He had been afraid to risk the road in the dark and now all he wanted was to wash up, take a nap, and then inspect the church. The church was all he had expected it to be. It dominated the village by the grandeur of its size and age. In fact, Larry had great hopes for Almas. He felt that, more than any village or town he had visited so far, Almas might possibly house the lost Child. His hands trembled as he reached for his bag, but he was determined not to betray by any sign or word the purpose of his visit. He had learned from experience that asking questions was useless and talking with people a waste of time.

The owner of the inn, Juan Ramírez, was used to renting one of his two rooms to an occasional salesman or tax man but only rarely to a tourist. The rooms were always ready, and Señora Ramírez, at the sight of a guest, would bring out her flowered china and begin to cook *paella* in a large copper pot. Juan Ramírez liked the fuss and excitement even more than the money that he would make from a guest. His profits came in regularly from the men of the village. They considered his bar more of a home than their own houses, and they left most of their pay there in exchange for the wine they drank. Whenever a guest was at the inn the talk inside the bar was animated, and Juan Ramírez was supposed to learn all about the visitor so that he could inform the men what business had brought him to Almas.

When greeting Larry Katchen at the door, Juan Ramírez had hoped that his guest was a talkative man, but to his question, "What brings you to this village?" he received a highly unsatisfactory answer.

"I'm interested in churches."

"Are you a religious man?" Juan Ramírez inquired.

Larry Katchen was surprised at the question. He had never thought of himself as either a religious or nonreligious man. He was, he thought, only a man with a mission, and his work fulfilled all his needs.

"I'm very tired and very dirty," he said, avoiding an answer. "Could you please show me to my room?" And that was the extent of their conversation.

By the time Juan Ramírez got back to the bar, he had evolved a theory about his strange and unexpected guest.

"He is an American ex-priest," he told the men at the bar.

"How do you know?"

"Did he tell you this himself?"

"He didn't have to," Juan declared, stroking his unshaved chin. "That he is an American I know from seeing his passport. That he was once a priest I can see in his eyes. He might not have been a Catholic, but he was a man of the cloth. He has lost God and is traveling around trying to find Him inside each church."

"What if he finds Him in Almas?" someone asked. "What will he do then? Will he stay here with us, or will he go back home and be a priest again?"

"If he finds God we'll have to drink his health."

"And the drinks will be on the house," someone laughed.

"We will have to wait and see," Juan Ramírez said gravely, not liking the jest about the drinks being on the house. "We'll just have to wait and see."

The men grew silent and listened, their heads up to hear the footsteps upstairs. The American paced for quite a while; then the bedsprings creaked and there were no more sounds.

"Do you know what I think?" asked the *alcalde*, Almas' mayor, who talked slowly and always asked if anyone wanted to learn what he had to say.

They waited for him to speak. They always did that; it was almost a game. They had many similar habits, based partly on respect but more on the wish not to change what seemed right to them.

"I think he may be a rich American," the mayor said, tapping his fat finger against the wood of the bar. No one said anything, doubting what they had heard. "And what's more," the mayor said, and paused to prolong the suspense, "he may be one of those who come to buy whole buildings and take them back."

That was too much for the cobbler, a swarthy man with gigantic hands. "Are you saying that he came all the way to Almas to buy our church and take it away with him to America? In that little car?"

"He may have been sent by someone," the mayor replied, tap-tapping on the bar twice. "Strange things like that happen with Americans. I hear they dismantle whole castles, taking each brick from the walls and marking it with a number. Once back in America, they put the bricks together so that the castle looks exactly as it did before."

Someone laughed; another coughed; two of the men shrugged their shoulders and downed their drinks. The mayor was a man of importance, yet he was not considered very bright. He had traveled to Sevilla, Córdoba, Grenada, and Málaga. Whenever he prepared to go anywhere, he would tell the men of the things he intended to demand for the village—a new road, a well, a factory that would give everyone, even the children, high-paying jobs. And when he came back he would tell of the things he had said, and to whom, and what the others had replied and sometimes promised. No one in Almas believed him anymore, even though they liked to listen to his dreams. They did not believe this story about castles but they said nothing, and the mayor went on, encouraged by their silence.

"If that should be the case, if the American were to take the church, there would be work for us all. A new road would certainly have to be built for the trucks that would come."

Upstairs, Larry Katchen could not sleep. He was lying in bed, looking out of the window at the twin spires of the big church of Almas.

He imagined, as he often did now, how it would be when he found the Child. He would come upon it suddenly, unexpectedly. It would not be hidden somewhere but rather it would be in plain view of everyone. The Child would be held by His Mother, a statue of no consequence, possibly even appalling in workmanship. For centuries the Child would have been held thus, and no one would ever have known that the Child was Angellini's. He would simply lift the Child and examine it to make sure, but he would know it at the very first sight.

The daydream ended there. He never thought beyond the discovery—of what would happen afterward.

It was afternoon when Larry Katchen finally set out for the church. He went first to the cemetery; it was his habit to look through the statues and grave markers before entering a church, for he liked to prolong the suspense, feed on the anticipation, and delay the final moment.

The cemetery of Almas was a triangular piece of ground, a fifteen-minute walk from the inn, on a plateau, treeless and windswept. Larry was followed there by a handful of children and two mangy dogs. The children did not speak to him nor to one another, but they watched his every move. He walked slowly through the graveyard. Most of the graves were marked simply with wooden crosses; some did not have even that much embellishment, but were outlined with small white stones. There were, however, three statues: one of Christ resurrected, with his hands outstretched, looking rather as if he had suddenly been struck blind; another of an angel kneeling; and a third of a figure bent down with grief, the face covered by two elongated hands. None of them impressed Larry.

When he entered the church, the children waited outside on the steps. He stood for a while, getting used to the darkness. A young girl was on her knees scrubbing the marble steps that led to the altar. She was the only person inside the church.

The statues of the saints were what he had expected, plaster copies of uninspiring originals. He had seen some of the early artworks that had been rescued from the church of Almas, in museums or reproduced in books. But what had been there in the fourteenth and fifteenth centuries had been replaced long ago. Most of the present statues were clothed in dresses of velour and satin, a custom Larry had deplored in an article he had written once for a rather obscure art journal.

His hopes were disappearing fast as he walked around the church. The only statue holding a child was a very ordinary Madonna. For the first time since he had started on his search, Larry Katchen felt close to despair. His quest seemed hopeless. His money was giving out, and soon he would have covered all the likely places in Spain.

The girl cleaning the altar steps got off her knees and, holding the bucket in one hand, disappeared behind the altar. She, at least, Larry thought, has accomplished what she set out to do, while I am accomplishing nothing at all. He felt old and tired.

What would become of him in his old age, he

wondered. Would he die alone as he had lived—friendless, with no one to remember him? Had he lived a normal life, working at a job, he would be retiring now, perhaps with a pension and savings. What had he done with his life? He had never been in love. He would not leave children, just a few dusty books. What claim, what excuse, could he make for all those years—that he had been a scholar, questing after his own Holy Grail?

For the first time, sitting in this gloomy church, he began to regret his past life. Larry Katchen was not used to such thoughts. Suddenly it seemed to him that he had spent a lifetime protecting himself against them—against people, against reality. But he could no longer deny the cold facts of waste, of insignificance, of evasions. The chill of dejection was in his bones and, for once, Larry Katchen came close to praying. After all, he thought as he looked up toward the great cross, it was for You that I've been searching.

chapter nine

She was sitting on the floor, the bucket of water beside her. The marble Child was in her arms, and the colored lights from the stained-glass window spilled around them. She had brought the Child a gift, a satin coverlet from a chalice. It was red, with threads of gold, and she covered the Child's shoulders with the cloth and smiled at its smiling face. Each day she brought a gift—a flower, a stone, a small mirror, a bead, or a ribbon, but today was different. Today, for the first time, she had stolen something from the sacristy, and she was both scared and happy about it.

What she wanted most of all was to be able to take the marble Child outside into the sun's brightness. Although she knew it could not feel the wind nor see the clouds, she wanted to do for it what she had done for the real child. But she could not make the secret of its existence known. She was certain, although she did not know why, that if anyone were to see it, it would be taken away from her, as the other child had been taken from her. She could not risk that. She would deny the world rather than lose this Child. Silently, she told all this to the marble figure and hoped it understood that it was not altogether her fault that she had to keep it hidden.

Out of the box in which she kept them, she took the gifts she had given the Child and spread them on the floor. One by one she touched them, trying to decide what they would play with today. She chose the mirror. By turning it toward the window's light she could catch a colored beam and make it dance on the church wall.

Larry Katchen was getting up to leave when he saw the rainbow of color shoot from behind the altar and fall on the granite of the wall. It jumped and skipped, then seemed imprisoned for a moment in a shaft of brightness and remained lifeless. After a moment it came to life again and moved giddily across the statues and the paintings depicting the stations of the cross. At first he thought that a butterfly had gotten lost in the somber church. When he realized it was a beam of colored light, he thought that perhaps a jewel was catching the rays of the sun. But what made it move? Cautiously he walked toward the altar, surprised at the dryness of his throat and the loud beating of his heart.

The girl sitting on the floor was cradling something in her arms, but he could not see what it was because her long hair shielded it from his sight. And yet he was sure, although later he could not say if he had been made certain by a flash of intuition or by an explosion of hope, that she was holding his Child. He waited, trying to still his heart and to make his breathing soundless.

The girl played with the mirror until the rays of the sun moved away from the window. Then she wrapped the marble figure in a piece of satin, held it to her lips and placed it gently, along with a small box, in a triangular hole at the bottom of the altar.

The girl got off her knees, and with her back to Larry, picked up the bucket of water and her mop and walked away. When he could no longer see her or hear her steps, he moved hurriedly toward the hiding place.

He had not expected that he would cry, but he was aware of his tears and impatiently rubbed them away with his sleeve before they could fall on the Child. The statue was without flaw, undamaged as he had hoped it would be, and it was more beautiful than in all his daydreams. Angellini had endowed the Child with truly human characteristics. It looked like a fat, loved, and happy baby. On its instep the artist had carved his initial, a rounded "A." In his gladness, Larry Katchen laughed.

By the time he had returned the statue to its hiding place, Larry Katchen had made an important decision. He would stay in Almas. He would live here and work on his next book, a book that would have as its subject the odyssey of the Child, its theft in Italy, its journey to Spain, and its discovery. Although the account could not be entirely factual, Larry, with a shiver of new excitement, was ready to fictionalize it, concentrating on the motives of those who had stolen the Child.

His mind raced with thoughts. He would help, if his help was needed and wanted, to keep Angellini's Child in the village of Almas. The Vatican Gallery, where it rightfully belonged, was full of treasures; this village had none. Thousands of art lovers would come to this forsaken place to see his discovery. It would not be easy for them to come, for the trip would demand devotion and sacrifice. But the people who came would be of the kind he admired most—the determined, devoted, serious art lovers, not the ordinary sightseers who hurried thoughtlessly from place to place.

Larry left the church. He must find the priest and tell him of the discovery of the Child.

The door of the parish house was opened by the girl who had been playing with the statue, and Larry Katchen felt a twinge of guilt. Was she going to be deprived of her only toy, he wondered, but he immediately dismissed such an irreverent idea. Providence or luck had prevented the girl from dropping and damaging the statue; now measures would have to be taken to insure its safety.

She led him silently through a corridor and into the priest's study. Before he could thank her she had gone, closing the heavy door behind her. Alone, he became aware of the weakness of his knees, the feeling of giddiness still with him. He waited impatiently for the priest. This day had been so very long in coming. Could he now share his pride and happiness with another human being?

He hoped that the priest would make the job of sharing easy. He hoped for a pleasant, chubby country cleric who would want to celebrate the discovery with a glass of sherry and a lot of friendly back-slapping. But the man who entered the room looked as tortured as an El Greco portrait. He was tall and extremely thin, with eyes that burned with a fire, or perhaps a fever, that seemed not of the body but of the soul.

Even while introducing himself Larry felt uneasy, as if his very presence was an interruption, an invasion of the priest's privacy. He regretted that he had not brought the news of the Child first to the villagers, perhaps to the mayor, who in turn would have related it to the priest. But it was too late for that now.

"The statue is a most important discovery," Larry was saying; yet his words sounded unimportant. "It will prove a great blessing to the village. It will bring art lovers from all over the world."

"How did you find it?" the priest asked.

"The girl, the one who works for you, was playing with it behind the altar."

"It is as it should be. When He was born the animals saw Him first, and then the shepherds, and only later the kings."

As the priest spoke there was a sadness in his voice, and Larry knew that he did not really grasp the importance of the find. Impatiently, he told him of Angellini, of his own long search for the missing figure and of his books, but even as he talked Larry thought angrily that he was not reaching the priest. He was failing in one of the few attempts he had ever made to communicate his passion, his excitement, to another human being. It was far easier for him to lecture to a hundred people than to talk privately to one person; he had always known this. As Larry turned to go, the priest's parting words confirmed the fact that he had only wasted his time by trying to share his happiness with another.

"The people of Almas need a living God most of all. To find Him they have to look for Him not in church but in each other."

The elation that Larry Katchen had felt slowly drained in the presence of the priest. Yet he was determined that his discovery be celebrated, not only by him but also by the people who would benefit from it, the villagers of Almas. He decided to make his next stop at the bar of the inn.

A handful of men stopped talking as he entered, and looked at him with respectful curiosity. They had done little work that day, wating to see what the stranger would do, and who would be proved right, Juan Ramírez or the *alcalde*.

Larry Katchen ordered a glass of sherry and asked where he might find the mayor of Almas.

"You need look no further than your elbow," the mayor said, and laughed nervously. Strangers always made him uneasy. Each time he left Almas he was seized by panic. Each time he talked to a man he did not know, he felt stiff with a fear that made him sweat and made his tongue stammer helplessly. But this foreigner was on his home ground. What reason was there to fear him?

There were formal introductions. Then Larry Katchen addressed the assembled men. He spoke slowly, looking at each man in turn. Their rugged faces expressed only curiosity at first, and then disbelief. But as they grasped the importance of Larry's news, there were murmurs of approval, and the excitement in their eyes made Larry very happy.

Much shouting, drinking, and long toasts filled the afternoon. When the hunchback came in for his daily glass of wine, they told him of the discovery, and he immediately wanted to share in it.

"I have known for a long time," he said loudly, "about the Child. As a matter of fact, during my first year at the church, I discovered the hiding place, that wooden plank."

Most of the men laughed, not believing the hunchback, but not Larry Katchen.

"What did you think of the statue when you first saw it?" he asked excitedly. He wanted to know how this strange and primitive man had reacted to Angellini's work.

"What did I think of it?" The hunchback repeated the question twice and scratched his head.

"Well, I thought it was the Christ Child."

The men laughed uproariously and some of them called out:

"He's a philosopher, that one!"

"An art critic!"

"He also discovered America, not only the statue."

The hunchback was well used to being laughed at, but he resented it now in the presence of the stranger.

"I certainly knew," he said not so loudly, "that it was a great work of art."

Larry Katchen smiled at the little man, and the hunchback felt better. He began to wonder if there might not be a reward attached to the finding of the statue. But he didn't dare ask about that.

By nightfall, they had begun to worry about the safety of the statue and decided that it should not be left where it was. The local carpenter offered to build a glass-encased receptacle which could be placed in front of the altar railing, where the statue might easily be seen by the expected multitudes. In the meantime, the mayor suggested, the Child should be put inside an old iron safe in the parish house.

From the inn the news spread rapidly throughout the village. Those who heard it declared the discovery a miracle. People gathered in small groups, merged into larger ones and separated to come together again. Laughter echoed through Almas' streets, and the cries of happiness were like songs, heard deep into the night.

Women wept and hugged their sleepy children, talking to them of the future, of the school that would be built, of the clothes they would have, of the opportunities that would make their youth golden, of the end of hopelessness. Men spoke soberly of the roads that would have to be built, of sewers, of hotels, of souvenirs that could be sold to the art lovers who would come to Almas, of the work that would have to be done and the pay that would be received, of the leisure they would have, and of the possessions that they would now be able to acquire. And some of them silently gave thanks to God for the change that would come— for the end to this dark, lonely poverty.

By nightfall the village seemed enveloped in a rain of gold: golden dreams, golden talk, golden possibilities. There was not so much greed in their wants and their plans as a great, bursting joy that came from the knowledge that, as despair died, hope was born.

And everyone in Almas that night, except the

deaf-and-dumb girl who knew nothing of what
had happened, was aware that tomorrow, for
once, would not be like yesterday.

chapter ten

On Sundays the girl did not work. Early in the
morning, she would take a basket with bread and
cheese and walk away from the village to the hills
to sit, as she used to, and watch the clouds and
feel the wind. On those long, solitary days she
thought of many things, of her father whom she
had not seen since she left home, of her grandfather who, unbeknown to her, had died in the
meantime, of the baby she had taken care of. Her
memories, her past, did not disturb her, but the
events of her present life were confusing and made
her wonder.

Why did Carmen avoid her? Why had she never
combed her hair again? That day, when Carmen
talked to her, the girl felt she had found a friend,
someone who would be close when she needed

closeness, someone who would look at her and smile and touch her. She had thought of putting up her hair herself the way she had seen Carmen do it, but she had decided against it. If her hair were left loose, Carmen might comb it for her again. But she never did.

In many little ways the girl tried to please the woman. She often would finish tasks that Carmen was performing; she would take a flower from the altar and place it by her bedside; she would help herself to the worst piece of meat or fish and leave the best for Carmen; she would refuse sweet bread so that Carmen would have enough for herself. But none of these gestures evoked a response. Since that day, Carmen had avoided the girl as much as possible, had not looked at her, had even stopped teaching her how to do the chores around the house.

It was almost the same with the priest. One day the girl had picked up a book from the priest's library and looked through it, finding it full of pictures. He had entered the room and found her, and the girl had felt ashamed of being caught, but he had smiled and taken down a large book from a higher shelf. He motioned her to a table and showed her the pictures in the book. They were all of mothers and children and she had eagerly gestured toward the church, telling him in her way that they showed the same woman and child whose statue was inside the church. And he had nodded his head and smiled at her.

She went to the library often, but since that one time the priest had not paid any attention to her. She wanted so much to be shown, to be taught. Even as a small child, learning a new chore had filled her with pride, and each discovery had made her happy. The two people she lived with now could teach her so very much, but each had turned away from her. Was it her fault? If so, what had she done to displease them?

If it were not for the marble Child, her life would be empty and sad. But now she could love the Child, and that made a great difference. She pretended again that it was not just a statue but a living, breathing thing. She closed her eyes and imagined she was holding it in her arms, here on the hillside, while the wind whipped the sparse grass. She smiled, thinking how it would laugh if it could only see the clouds painting white images in the sky. And for a while she forgot her loneliness.

On this Sunday, while the girl spent the morning in the hills, the villagers of Almas gathered in the church for a Mass of thanksgiving. The priest spoke solemnly of the danger in regarding Angellini's Child only as a material treasure. "It is a statue of the Infant Jesus," he said, "and we must always be aware that it represents our Saviour. It was He who taught us the Way of the Cross—the only way that leads to Him."

After the services there was again much shouting and laughing, as people shared their dreams with one another. There was dancing and the sound of songs, guitars, and castanets. In the afternoon, the men gathered at the bar to discuss the changes that would come to Almas.

"I shall go to Madrid," declared the *alcalde*, "and demand that a new road be built to Almas."

The men nodded, and for once they believed him.

"And we will need sewers, and a new well."

"And a hotel for the tourists!"

Juan Ramírez, the innkeeper, frowned.

"Almas already has a hotel. This inn can be enlarged."

"We'll need a skyscraper for those who come to see the Child," someone said. "A thousand rooms."

"I'll add rooms," Juan Ramírez said firmly. But the men continued to joke among themselves and insist that Almas deserved a real hotel, until Juan Ramírez grew angry and began to serve them soured wine.

The women talked about the new shops that Almas would have, and about the things they would buy with the money earned from the tourist trade. Then someone remembered the girl.

"If it were not for the deaf-and-dumb girl, the statue would never have been discovered."

"The devil's power must have left her when she went to work for the priest."

"Sometimes that happens," an old woman said. "God sometimes turns evil people into miracle-workers or saints."

"We must give credit to the girl."

"I will do more than that," the mayor's wife said. "I will give her one of my old dresses."

"And I will give her my shawl. My old black shawl will keep her warm against the winter winds."

"She could use some shoes. I have a new pair and my old ones are still not worn out."

The women gathered their gifts and walked to the parish house. When Carmen opened the door, they asked to see the girl.

"What do you want with her?" Carmen demanded. She did not care for any of the village women. They had husbands and families. She felt that none of them could possibly know the kind of emptiness and despair with which she had had to live.

"We brought her some gifts," the mayor's wife said.

"We want to thank her. It was she who discovered the statue."

"She knows nothing of that," Carmen said, angry with them, angry with herself because she could not share their excitement or their dreams.

"It does not matter what she knows," the mayor's wife said haughtily. "She deserves our thanks."

Suddenly the girl appeared at Carmen's side, her hair loose from her morning on the hillside, her eyes surprised and a little frightened. She did not understand why the women of the village were giving her gifts, why their hands patted her hair, why kindness was in their eyes. When the women left, the girl looked in wonder at the things spread on the kitchen table.

"It was you who changed their lives," Carmen said and looked away. "Nothing will ever again be the same in Almas. Only for us will nothing change. We are not a part of them."

But there was another person in Almas that Sunday who felt left out and alone. Although the villagers had come to shake his hand, although he had been invited to eat and drink with them, Larry Katchen felt himself withdraw. As the day wore on, he grew more and more depressed. Now that the statue had been found, it seemed to him that the most important part of his life was spent. He began to doubt that he could live in Almas, that he could write the book about the statue's theft.

He felt impatient and angry with himself at not being able to share in the happiness of the villagers. He had waited so long for the discovery of the Child, and now his future seemed very dark. His quest had been like a part in a play. The role had come to an end, and he had been asked to leave the stage.

chapter eleven

When the girl went to the church on Monday afternoon as usual, she was surprised to find a group of men standing in front of the altar, where a large case of wood and glass was being erected. She went about her chores quietly, but a sense of disaster went with her. She was afraid to look toward the altar: someone might have wandered there and found her Child. She worried that she might not have replaced the wooden plank carefully.

More people came into the church later, summoned by bells the girl could not hear. Frightened, she hid behind the recess of a side altar. Outside, a procession was approaching from the parish house. The priest held the Child high. He was followed by the mayor holding a large candelabra, the candlelight disappearing in the blaze of the autumn sun. Ten choirboys came next, and closing the ranks walked Larry Katchen holding a velvet pillow on which the statue was to rest in its case. They entered the church.

Long after the people had gone and the lights had been put out, the girl emerged from her hiding place and walked to the main altar. At first she tried to keep her eyes away from the wooden case, but when she was close she looked inside. By the dim candlelight she saw her Child lying on a red velvet cushion, turned to one side, its blind eyes looking down the long nave.

She raised a clenched fist and brought it down hard against the glass. She did not feel pain; she did not know that blood from a gash in her hand stained her dress. Carefully she lifted the Child and wrapped it in her dust cloth. At the side door she hesitated. Should she go into the house to take the shawl and the shoes the women had given her? No, those things did not really belong to her. The only thing that belonged to her was the Child.

She walked slowly, turning around from time to time to see if anyone was following her. When she reached the peak of the first hill, she looked back for the last time. Almas was bathed in purple light, and the mountains beyond dimmed to the falling night. She began to run across an olive grove, pursued by her streaming hair.

The dusk made the olive trees pale, and the evening breeze made the leaves shimmer like frightened fish. Tongues of dew brushed wetness against her legs. A bush scratched at her dress, but she ran on. The dark of night came fast. A parchment crest of the moon shed no light and the stars were frozen in the dark blue sky. She held the Child more tightly. In fear and uncertainty she walked more slowly now, more carefully, as the blind might walk over an unknown land.

By midnight she could walk no longer. She sat down on a rock, placing the Child in her lap. She did not hear the barking of dogs from a nearby village, but fear made her shiver as much as the cold. She tried to tell herself there was nothing to be afraid of, that the Child was safe with her; they would be safe together. But even the rocks seemed shadowed with a terror she could not hear, nor see, nor understand.

But all the nameless fears she felt were not as strong as the fear of having to give back the Child. She got up and began to walk again. She was guided by the brightest of the low stars, and she walked surely as if a straight road lay in the middle of the fields and across the hills. All night she walked. At dawn she saw a line of forest ahead, and she knew that she had come far from the village of Almas.

With the coming of light the girl felt elated. The marble Child, warmed by her arms, seemed real. She pretended that it also could see what she was seeing for the first time: tall trees that roofed the sky with green and glimmers of light. The forest reminded her of the village church. It was cool, serene, and peaceful. The moss under her feet was soft and moist, and she knelt down to touch its silkiness. Then she lay down, placing the marble Child in the crook of her arm.

When she awoke the forest was getting darker, and she knew that she had to find food and shelter before the night. She walked on as straight as the pathless forest would allow. Several times she stopped to eat blueberries. Once she saw a deer grazing quietly, as though suspended in time and space. She stood still until it came alive and moved on, its body long and graceful, its white tail like a lost cloud. By the time the light had reddened with the setting sun, she came upon a trail and followed it, and just before nightfall she saw a clearing and in it a little hut.

For a while the girl did not dare to approach the hut. She waited, watching from behind a tree for any movement beyond the closed windows and the door. The hut was built of rough wood, with a chimney of fieldstones. A stream of clear water flowed in a crescent around it on three sides. Nothing moved, and so she went nearer.

The door of the hut opened easily at her touch, and she walked inside its only room. There was a pile of wood and kindling by the large fireplace. Near the window on a table was a kerosene stove and several cans of food. A low bed was covered by a bearskin rug, and another animal skin was thrown over the only chair. The girl smiled at the Child in her arms. They had found a home at last.

She slept late the next day, for the sun did not penetrate the roof of the trees to awaken her. When she opened her eyes, she did not know where she was. She had dreamed that she walked through green fields where white birds flew about. In the dream she heard, for the first time, songs and voices and the rustling of wings. And there were children in her dream, walking hand-in-hand with her among the grass. The children laughed and she had laughed with them, and she could hear the sound of her own laughter.

She bathed herself and the marble Child in the cold stream and then found a patch of sunlight and placed the Child on her lap. They sat all morning in the autumn warmth. In the afternoon she gathered berries, and found mushrooms growing in the carpet of dead leaves and cooked them on the stove.

No one came except the deer. She saw them that afternoon, drinking from the stream, pausing to listen and look. And they did not run away when she quietly opened the cabin door. But when they did flee, they seemed to take with them the very daylight.

She hoped to be able to stay at the hut forever. It would be peaceful here and safe. She would wake up each day at dawn and go to sleep before dark. Here she would have all that she needed: shelter, enough food, the sun, and her Child.

Her Child. Slowly the girl began to realize how much she had come to depend on the Child as an object of her love. She knew now that to live she had to give love. But love, like a gift, must be accepted. She had tried giving love to people, to her father and grandfather, to Carmen and to the priest, but they did not want it. She had given love to the sick baby, but the baby had died. She had now the one thing that would not refuse her love, her marble Child.

This realization swept over the girl like the sun breaking through the trees, warm and real, a single light illuminating her whole being. And for the first time in her life she was glad to be who she was.

part
three

---

the
hunt

Yo me asomé a un precipicio
por ver lo que había dentro,
y estaba tan negro el fondo,
que el sol me hizo daño luego.

—Ferran

[I leaned over an abyss
to see what was below,
and it was so dark down there
that afterward the sun hurt my eyes.]

chapter twelve

The hunchback hated the morning. He hated to wake up from his dreams, and he hated to get out of bed. He slept rolled up into a ball, with his head tucked between his arms, his knees reaching his chin, convinced that, because of this position, he always dreamt long, exciting dreams. But he had to be in the sacristy by five-thirty every morning to prepare for the six o'clock Mass.

"Why do you say Mass so early?" he often asked the priest. "In Seville, where you come from, Father, that might be the right hour. But in Almas, in a village church, a seven or even an eight o'clock Mass would be much better."

"Wasn't there always a six o'clock Mass before I came?" the priest asked.

"Yes, but the priest before you," the hunchback said, "was not a learned man. His ignorance made him want to say Mass that early in the day. But you, Father—you are a man of intellect. And besides, who comes to your daily Mass?"

The priest, embarrassed, did not reply.

"You and I know, Father, that there will never be anyone but those five women," the hunchback said. "The five who have nowhere to go and nothing to do all day. If you were to say Mass at noon they would be here. They are getting older each year. They too could use some sleep, just as you and I."

But the daily Mass remained at six and the hunchback could only mutter to himself about the five women.

"Five crows! Won't they ever die, or even get sick? Each day for eighteen years they have come. Even eighteen years ago, when I first began to work here, they were old. Maybe they're not human. Maybe they've always been here, since the beginning of time. It does no good talking to them. 'We like coming to Mass at six.'" He curled his lips in imitation of their smiles and spoke to himself in a high-pitched, whining voice.

The hunchback was laying out the priest's vestments. He poured wine and water into cruets, took the paten, chalice, and purifier out of the old chest and placed them on the sacristy table, and was going out to light the candles as the priest came through the door.

The women had not yet entered the church. They usually arrived together just as the hunchback started to ring the bell, and they stayed after Mass, praying for the almost forgotten sins of their youth, their arms spread wide in the shape of the cross, their heads tilted back, their lips moving fast with prayers they had learned on their mothers' knees. They would leave the church together, only to come back for the benediction in the afternoon. "My honor guard," the priest had once described them in a letter to his widowed sister.

The hunchback lit the two wax candles, turned on the light over the altar, and looked toward the newly-erected receptacle for the statue of the Child.

He would have had the case made of gold, if he had been the one to make the decision. And he would not have placed it there until he was able to fill the church with important people from all over the world. He would have invited kings and queens and, of course, the Pope. He had been appalled at the small procession yesterday. He had expected at least a little pomp, but there was none at all, just the villagers summoned by his bells, and a few people from neighboring communities. It had been a wasted opportunity as far as he was concerned.

He wanted to see how the statue looked on its velvet cushion. Without him not even that much would have been done. The cushion had been mouldering in the sacristy, and he himself had brought it to the priest with the suggestion that it be used for the Child. He had expected the priest to ask him to carry the cushion into the church, but the foreigner had been chosen for the job.

He heard the glass crunch under his feet before he saw the destruction: the wood splintered, the red cushion covered with sharp pieces of glass, stains of blood on the floor, and the Child gone.

The priest was putting on the chasuble as the hunchback rushed into the sacristy.

"Lord," the priest prayed, "Who didst say 'My yoke is sweet and my burden light,' grant that I may so bear it as to obtain Thy grace." When the prayer was finished the priest looked at the hunchback's excited face. "What is it, Carlos?" he asked.

"The Child is gone!"

It seemed to the priest that God had punished him as swiftly as he had sinned, for as he was saying the words of the prayer he had been thinking that Angellini's statue, instead of being a blessing to the villagers, would cause them to commit sins of greed and pride.

"It's been stolen," the hunchback shouted, his long face red with emotion. "The glass is broken and the statue has disappeared!" Suddenly a thought struck him and he lowered his voice. "The foreigner! It must have been the foreigner!"

Could it be an act of God? The thought flashed through the priest's mind. A sign of His Divine Love had been perverted by greed, and God had taken His gift away.

"I never trusted him," the hunchback said loudly now. "I never trusted the foreigner." He hoped the priest would agree that the foreigner was the thief. But the priest said nothing and the hunchback grew impatient. "What should we do? Should I close the church door?"

"Oh, no!" the priest said. "We will pray for our sins."

"There will be time for prayer after we find the Child," the hunchback said angrily, not understanding why the priest did not give him any orders. "We should forget about the Mass," he said. "We should go after the foreigner."

"The Mass will be celebrated," the priest said. "Go ring the bell."

"But, Father, what about the Child and the thief?"

The priest said nothing. The hunchback hobbled away. He was furious and did not go to ring the bell. Since the priest would not act, he had to act himself. He thought of alerting the village to the theft. He saw himself going from house to house, waking the people with cries of distress, moving from door to door like a messenger of doom. But it was more important to find the foreigner, to take the statue away from him, by force if need be, and bring it back to the church. He would do all that alone. The people would remember him, even long after his death, for his courage.

He was happy to see that the American's old car was still in front of the inn. A crafty thief, the hunchback decided, never runs until he must. He had probably hidden the statue among his belongings in the leather suitcase, and no one would dare to look for it. No one except him.

He opened the door of the inn as quietly as the creaking wood would allow. Juan Ramírez' wife was on her knees, scrubbing the floor in front of the bar. He could not get past her without being seen. He tried to remember if there was a back way he could use to get upstairs to the guest rooms. But it was too late. She had seen him.

"What do you want?" the innkeeper's wife shouted at him. She always spoke to him loudly, as if she thought him deaf. He didn't like her for that and for the look of contempt in her eyes. "You're bringing in dirt. Get out of here."

He thought fast. "Where is the milk?" he asked. "I came for the priest's milk."

"Carmen comes for the milk," the woman said. "What happened to her? Is she dead? And what's the matter with you? Why didn't you ring the bell?"

His act of courage would be ruined if she knew why he had come. He did not want her to interfere with what he had decided to do alone. He couldn't let her suspect that anything was wrong.

"Didn't you hear the bell?" he said. "I rang the bell as always. Now I must get the milk."

The woman got off her knees, muttering, and rubbed her red hands against her apron. "You just stay right where you are," she said peevishly. "Don't move. You've already brought in dirt that I must clean up again. Next time Carmen sends you for the milk come around to the back like she does."

When she went through the door leading to the kitchen the hunchback tiptoed up the stairs. His mind was now full of images of a fight and capture, and of a trial in Córdoba with himself as the star-witness and accuser. He was aware of a lightness in his head and of sweating, and he would have sung out his excitement, or at least laughed from the happy dizziness that he felt, but he didn't dare make a sound.

Larry Katchen slept with his mouth slightly open. His suitcase, with its lid open, was on the only chair. The hunchback stopped in the middle of the room. Another idea had come to him. If the foreigner was an American, he would be rich. What would he be willing to pay to have nothing at all said about the theft? How much more would he give the hunchback if he helped him escape? What could the value of the statue be? A million pesetas? Two million? More?

He moved closer to the suitcase to get a better look at the Child. His joy was now marred by his worry of being cheated. People always took advantage of him, and life itself had dealt unfairly with him from his birth. As he rummaged inside the suitcase, it fell with a clatter to the floor and the foreigner sat up in bed and stared at the hunchback with confused eyes.

"What is it?" he asked in a tongue the hunchback didn't understand. Then, fully awake, he asked the same question more loudly, in Spanish this time.

The hunchback smiled craftily and said nothing but looked toward the suitcase on the floor.

"What do you want?" Larry Katchen was shouting now. "What are you doing here?"

"I came for the Child," the hunchback said slowly and grinned. He wanted to catch the man off guard. If the statue were hidden, the man's eyes would dart to it. Carlos suspected that the man was more than a match for him; he must look and act with more authority, he decided.

Suddenly he remembered an incident he had almost forgotten. A few years ago a farmer had lost several of his chickens and the police had questioned everyone in Almas. Two policemen had come from Córdoba, one dressed in a uniform and the other in plain clothes. When it had been the hunchback's turn to be questioned, he had been immensely impressed with the uniformed policeman. The man had held his hands behind his back, his legs spread wide, and he had talked from under his nose with his head lowered, his voice deep and menacing so that it sent shivers down the hunchback's spine.

The hunchback now assumed this same stance and lowered his head until his chin rested on his chest. When he spoke his voice was deep and, he hoped, as frightening as the policeman's had been. "I am talking about the statue of the Child you've stolen from the church," he said. "You stole it, probably last night, and you've hidden it away. It is not in your suitcase. Where is it then?" The stance must have impressed the foreigner for he got out of bed and stood attentively in front of the hunchback.

"Tell me! Has the statue been stolen?" Larry Katchen's voice was intense. "Is the Child really gone?"

The hunchback laughed.

"Playing the innocent won't get you anywhere," he said triumphantly. "I know that you stole it."

Larry Katchen began to dress. If the statue of the Child was indeed missing, he thought, his life would be as it had been before. Once more there would be the quest, the anticipation, the planned activity. He had gone to bed drained of all desire to waken. But now the familiar sense of excitement filled his mind. The only necessity of his life, he realized, was a planned tomorrow. Without that he had no life.

"I would be willing not to report the theft to the authorities. I might even arrange for you to get out of Almas without anyone knowing anything."

The hunchback spoke slowly and his words reechoed as if he had said them to an empty room. Even as he talked, he knew the foreigner was not listening to him.

It was no use. Things would always be as they were. Nothing could possibly change. As always, he had failed. The American was no thief, and he himself was no hero. There would be no capture, no trial, no fame. The statue had disappeared and it would never be found. The dreams would have to end. Nothing, and no one, would ever change the misfortune, the misery, the poverty, and the hopelessness that were part of everyone's life in Almas.

chapter thirteen

The sin the priest had always been most concerned about, and most powerless against, was the sin of distraction. He had never been able to chain down his thoughts. As a young man, his thoughts had always been of God and the chain had not been necessary. But now his thoughts veered off in unknown directions and sprouted under-thoughts, subterranean mazes in which he felt lost. It seemed to the priest that as a youth he had seen clearly the way which would lead to his soul's salvation, but as he grew older he often found himself in a wilderness with few trails.

All through the Mass the priest tried not to think about the missing statue, but each time he turned from the altar to face the congregation, he would see the five women staring, as if hypnotized, at the smashed case.

The idea that God took the statue from the village in anger, in revulsion against the materialistic thoughts of the villagers, grew and became a certainty. Why couldn't the village have rejoiced in its find in a spiritual way? Why could they not accept the statue as a sign of God's love? Why did they have to build dreams of worldly gain within the domain of God?

But had it not always been like that? Were not the Christians often guilty of perverting the teachings of Christ? "My kingdom is not of this world," He had said. Yet there had been an Inquisition; there had been countless religious persecutions—all in His Name! What divine sign would satisfy them? Was there no hope at all for the people of Almas, or for Man?

In the sacristy, after Mass, the priest deplored his thoughts. If the people of Almas were not closer to God it was surely his fault, and his fault alone. He did not really know the people whose shepherd he was supposed to be, and yet he had condemned them. In his three years in Almas he had spoken to them only from the pulpit in words they probably did not understand, and of things that were a million light-years removed from their daily preoccupations. And what of those daily pre-

113

occupations. He had not shared in them. He had gone to their homes only when someone was very ill, dying, or dead. And he had never comforted them as a man, only as a priest. Such comfort was not enough. The poverty of their bodies affected their minds, yet he had done nothing to enrich their minds. Instead of isolating himself with his books, he should have helped the people. He could have started a school. He could have done so many things.

"Who might have stolen it? And why?"

These words startled the priest, and he turned to see who spoke them. The American was standing in the doorway of the sacristy.

"Is there anyone in the village," Larry Katchen was asking, "who is an atheist perhaps, or your enemy? Who hates the church enough to have done it out of revenge?"

"I don't know," the priest said. "I don't know them at all."

The words rang loudly in his ears, and the truth of the words was ugly. If only he could start his life in Almas over again. If only he had felt at the beginning what he was feeling now—tolerance, love, and a desire to help the people—to make up for the things he had never done. If only he could find the statue and give it back to them. He would no longer worry about what it meant to the villagers. They had a right to dream of better lives.

"We must do everything we can to find it," he said to the American.

Looking at the empty receptacle they tried to guess why anyone would take the Child and what might have happened to it. Larry Katchen was outraged by the deed. But the priest was only obsessed with the idea that his indifference to the need of the villagers could only be atoned for by his returning the marble Child to the church.

"Father!"

Carmen was standing in front of them, her face worried. She was looking at the priest and had not noticed the damaged receptacle.

"What is it?"

"The girl is gone. She didn't sleep in her room last night."

The priest looked at Larry Katchen. They both knew who had taken the statue now.

"She must have considered it her own," Larry said. "When she saw it in the case, she just took it and ran away. Where could she be?"

The priest was not listening. He was giving thanks to God that it had been the girl. The girl would do the statue no harm, and she would be easy to find.

"The villagers will never forgive her," Carmen said, shuddering.

"Is she an orphan?" Larry Katchen asked.

"No, she has a father," Carmen said, "but she would not have gone to him."

"Why not?"

"She was born deaf and dumb. Her father disowned her long ago."

"But he might know," Larry began impatiently, "he might know where she may have taken the statue."

"I will fetch him," Carmen said, "but he will tell you nothing. She does not interest him."

The priest did not hear them. His thoughts were in the future. God, in His Infinite Mercy, was giving him a chance to become a real priest to the people of the village. And this time he was determined not to let the opportunity go to waste.

The village of Almas awakened to the news of the statue's disappearance. At first there was disbelief and uneasy laughter, but when the news was confirmed again and again by the five women who had been to the early Mass, some of the villagers became frightened.

"We are truly cursed," they said.

They gathered in groups as they had the night

before, but now no one smiled and there was defeat in their faces.

"Our future is gone with the statue," a villager said, and many agreed that all they could do was to accept this calamity.

"It's our fate to be poor," they said. "We cannot change what must be."

Some went into the church to see for themselves. A few stayed to pray, but others came out cursing their fate. And a few wondered silently how they could ever have believed that anything good would happen to them. Even the children seemed to sense that something was terribly wrong.

"Who could have done it?" was the question most often asked.

"I am sure the thief is the foreigner," the hunchback told a group of men.

"But he is still here. Besides, he was the one who found the statue. Why would he take it without telling anyone? It doesn't make sense."

"Nothing makes sense," the hunchback replied. "All I know is that I questioned him and looked inside his suitcase. But he is clever. Right now he is with the priest, and God only knows what lies he is telling."

Suddenly, the hunchback's depression turned to anger.

"Why do we stand around, doing nothing?" he shouted. "Why don't we question the foreigner and the priest? Why don't we act?"

The mayor appeared in the crowd, hurriedly buttoning his shirt.

"I agree," he said in his most solemn voice. "Without the statue there will be no progress, no new road, no improvements of any kind. No tourists will come to Almas."

"But what can we do?" a man asked.

"The thief must be apprehended. I shall call the police in Córdoba," the mayor announced.

"Who needs them?" the hunchback shouted. "It is our statue and we can get it back ourselves!"

Now he had their attention again. They were watching him and listening, waiting for him to tell them what to do.

"Let us demand an answer from the priest and the foreigner," he said. "No one shall take away what is ours!"

"Well-spoken!" someone cried.

"To the parish house!"

They advanced, with the hunchback leading the way. He climbed the steps of the house and turned to look at the crowd. Their faces, raised to him, were respectfully attentive. For once they listened to him. Whatever else might happen, he would always remember this day. He knocked hard against the door.

The priest's face was pale as he opened the door, but he was smiling and not many of the villagers had ever seen his smile.

"It's been found!" someone whispered.

The hunchback spoke loudly so that everyone would hear. "We've come to ask if the foreigner stole the Child."

"You should know better than that," the priest replied gently. He motioned for Larry Katchen to stand beside him. "This man is a guest in our village. It was he who discovered our treasure, and he will help us get it back."

"We don't need his help," the hunchback shouted angrily.

The priest raised his hands. He spoke loudly.

"We think we know who has taken the statue and why. And shortly we will have it back where it belongs."

"Who is the thief?" someone in the crowd yelled, and the shout was taken up until it grew into a chant.

"We have the right to know," the hunchback cried. "Tell us the name of the thief!"

The priest smiled at the hunchback.

"Does it matter, Carlos?"

"We have the right to know!" the hunchback

repeated more loudly, and the priest was surprised by the anger in his face. Of all the villagers, he knew the hunchback best, and yet the man now acted as if they were enemies. Fists began to wave in the air, and frightened children clung to their mothers. The chanting grew and the crowd pressed closer to the steps.

"We want to know!"

"Tell us!"

"Who is the thief?"

Again the priest raised his hands.

"We should offer our thanks to God," he began.

"We need no sermons!"

"Don't tell us to pray!"

"He knows!"

"The priest is shielding the thief!"

Desperately, the priest tried to think of a way to win back their confidence. He had to prove himself their friend. He had to tell them.

"The deaf-and-dumb girl took the statue," he said at last.

For a moment there was silence. Then more angry shouts broke from the crowd.

"We will get the statue back," the priest said. "I have sent for the girl's father." But his voice was lost against their shouting.

In panic, the priest begged the crowd to keep calm. He told them that the girl was innocent, that she loved the Child, that no harm would come to the statue.

But nobody heard his words, and as he pleaded he grew afraid for the girl. Fear lodged in his heart, together with a feeling of great guilt. He should never have told them who had stolen the Child.

Now the girl's father was coming toward them.

"Here he is," the priest cried. "Here is Ramón de Prada!"

The people turned silently. They had not seen Ramón de Prada for some time. He had isolated himself completely, living a hermit's life, only tending his own fields and his animals. Now they were shocked at the way he looked. He had grown thin and bent, and he walked with the slowness of a man who has nowhere to go. He was unshaven and his hair had turned completely white. His eyes, once blue-green and bright, were now dull and colorless like the eyes of a blind man. The villagers stepped aside to let him pass. He stopped in front of the parish-house steps, but he did not look at the priest.

"Do you know where your daughter might be?" the priest asked.

"I have nothing to do with her," Ramón de Prada said, and his voice was full of resentment. "I did not teach her to steal. What do you want from me?"

The priest came down the steps but the man shrank away from the priest's hand.

"We want to find her and bring her back. We want to know where she might have gone."

"I do not know. The statue is yours, not mine. It would have made no difference in my life. You look for it." He turned his back on the priest and walked away.

For years Ramón de Prada had believed that his life ended when his wife died. He had made himself believe that her death had deprived him of any love he might ever have been able to feel. He had blamed his own daughter for her death. But now, as he walked down the deserted village street away from the angry voices, he knew it was all a lie. He had never had love to give. He had never felt love. He was barren of love, and his infirmity was greater than that of his deaf-and-dumb child. This was his sin; he must live with it. Even death, for which he waited as for the opening of a locked door, would not change what he was.

Hardly had he gone when the crowd began to murmur again. Some spoke loudly and angrily against the girl.

"We should never have trusted her," the mayor's wife said. "She repaid our kindness with treachery."

Now Carmen stepped forward. "What kindness have you shown her?" she demanded.

"We gave her things," the mayor's wife indignantly replied.

"I gave her my good shawl," a woman shouted from the crowd.

"And I, my shoes!"

"Your discarded things are where you left them," Carmen said. "She asked nothing from anyone." She turned on her heels and went inside the house, slamming the door behind her.

The priest raised his hands. He wished desperately to tell them that he was a changed man, that he would no longer just preach to them, but that now he also wanted to understand them. But they would not believe him yet. First he had to prove himself worthy of their trust.

"We will get the statue back," he shouted. "I'll find the girl, I promise you that. Go to your homes and wait."

"The girl is a witch!"

"She killed García's child!"

"She did not!" the priest shouted.

They turned their faces to him and he was frightened by the hatred in their eyes.

"Let's find her," the hunchback screamed from

the steps of the parish house. "Let's go after her and take the statue away!"

He picked up a stick and brandished it over his head.

"Follow me!" he shouted.

"I forbid you to go!" the preist cried.

But they did not hear him as they followed the hunchback down the street. They were a screaming mob now, beyond reason, beyond guilt. They were like that other mob, the priest thought, that screamed for a Crucifixion. And they too had their Judas: himself.

chapter fourteen

Larry Katchen watched the villagers and listened to them with growing fascination. It was the same kind of fascination with which, as a child, he had studied ants. He had moved the ants about, confused them, disrupted their lives by transporting them into strange surroundings. And he had stood over them, watching. His discovery of the statue seemed now to have the same effect on the villagers of Almas.

Larry had always deliberately limited his association with people. He had no friends because emotional attachments, he believed, upset the order of his life. People, as far as he was concerned, were the unstable elements in life: unlike books they could not be depended upon. Polite uninvolvement had always separated him from them. With that distance between himself and the world he had always been safe from commitments, and therefore untouched by disappointments.

Standing beside the priest, he had felt the emotional currents of hate, suspicion, and anger surge from the crowd, and the nakedness of these emotions had amazed and frightened him. He wished he could examine each one closely, as he would something tangible, under a microscope. But the feelings of the crowd were too mercurial to be held and studied. As Larry watched and listened, he felt drawn toward them, toward some inevitable course. And when the crowd moved, he ran after them.

Soon he was among them, part of them, running with them. For the first time in his life Larry Katchen felt that he belonged. For the first time in his life he was not alone. Someone had given him a stick, and he noticed that now everyone held a stone, a stick, or a pitchfork. Juan Ramírez had run into the inn and brought out a shotgun; its black barrel glistened whenever the sun came out from behind the clouds. The faces of the villagers, darkened by anger, reddened by shouts, were stark with a strength Angellini would have loved to sculpt, Larry Katchen thought. The crowd ran on.

Leaving the village road they were caught in

the narrowness of a path. And now they began to bump into each other and shove angrily as though they possessed a surplus of resentment to vent on one another. An old woman in black cried out as she fell. Someone cursed. A child wept and was scooped up by his mother who wanted to catch up with the others.

Almost at a trot they went up the hill, but soon the old people fell back, pushed aside by the young and the strong and the impatient ones. By the time they reached the hill's crest, there were two groups, the men in front, still led by the hunchback, the women and children and the old a few yards behind. And Larry Katchen was out front with the men.

The hunchback raised his hand like a general directing his troops, and signaled the men to spread in a wide line across the rocky hills. And suddenly Larry Katchen saw them as an army in a holy war.

Last night he had heard them talk of the future, and he had been appalled at the pettiness of their dreams. He had been angered by what his statue meant to them—a key to meager treasures. But here on the hillside it seemed to Larry that the villagers had changed—that now they sought the statue for itself.

They reached the rocky hills where Ramón de

Prada's sheep grazed. The animals lifted their heads and stared blankly at them. The wind whipped at their clothes and cooled their sweating faces. On a rock above, they saw Flora García's son, asleep. The hunchback raised his hand and motioned them to stop and, alone, advanced toward the boy. He climbed up to the rocky ledge and they saw him standing, outlined black against the cloudy sky, over the boy who was still asleep.

"Where is the girl?" they heard him shout.

The boy sat up and rubbed his eyes. He looked at the hunchback and at the crowd below.

"What happened?" he asked, terrified.

"He knows!" someone shouted.

"He's hidden them both!"

"He's protecting the girl, as his mother did!"

"Let's make the boy tell!"

They advanced with their weapons raised, climbing the rock, pushing and pulling, and their cries carried from hill to hill. The rays of the sun appeared briefly from behind a cloud, lighting up their features, and Larry Katchen saw, etched into their faces, a hunger for blood.

He turned and ran blindly down the slope, away from their shouts, away from their raised fists, away from what he had seen on their faces. Pure terror seized him as he realized that he had been one of them. They meant to kill the girl, but instead they would kill the boy! With their pagan, medieval minds, they had made themselves believe that they could exchange one life for another, so mortgaged was their reason to violence.

He ran, stumbling and falling, getting up to run faster, to put a greater distance between them and himself. Desperately he wanted to forget that he had almost joined them in the horrible ritual of death.

But what of the girl? If they found her, they would kill her too. He must protect her! He, himself, had put her in mortal danger. She had loved the statue, his statue! And he had taken it away from her. In his arrogant selfishness he was responsible for everything that had happened. It was too late to help the boy, but he could at least save the girl.

chapter fifteen

To the hunchback, the chase into the hills had been a journey of happiness. All his life people had either ignored him or impatiently dismissed him, as if the infirmity of his body had stretched to encompass his mind. His mind had always been wasted on cunning, on guessing what would please others. Each afternoon, in the village bar, he had to play the buffoon to obtain attention. Unless he said something funny or outrageous, the men turned their backs on him and, sometimes irritated by his mere presence, they waved him away.

Now suddenly everything had changed. As he led them his body seemed to have grown straight and tall, and the hump on his back was no longer a painful weight; it had ceased to exist. Maybe, the hunchback thought, a miracle had actually happened, and it was no longer there for them to see as it was no longer there for him to feel.

A sweet sensation of power and gratitude spread through him. Were it not for the job he had to do, he would cheerfully have paused to speak of it and to thank the people for it, for they were the ones responsible for his feeling. He was ashamed of the dislike he had felt for many of them in the past. Now, these same people, by the mere fact of following him, had become his friends. Their confidence was a gift, and he would return the gift by bringing the statue safely back to Almas' church.

When he saw the García boy sleeping on the rock, the hunchback realized this was his great opportunity to show the people how efficient he could be at questioning. There had been no one to watch him with the foreigner; maybe that was why he had failed. Now, with this crowd of friends at his back, he was sure he would be as impressive as the Córdoba policeman.

He had not meant to shout the first question so loudly; yet he did want to catch the boy off guard, to surprise and confuse him. The less time he had to think, the more likely he would be to tell the truth. But he did not really believe that the boy knew where the girl might be, or even anything about the statue's disappearance.

Suddenly, the others began to shout. He turned from the boy to see their faces distorted by an anger he himself did not feel. Why were they so angry? Why were they waving their fists and their sticks? Something had gone wrong.

"Stop!" he shouted.

But they did not listen. They were climbing up the rocks toward him and the boy, their faces coming closer, and he grew terribly afraid, but not for himself. It was the boy they wanted to hurt. But why?

"Let's make him tell!"

"Stop!" he shouted again.

He turned to the boy and saw how pale his face was. I will not let them hurt him, the hunchback thought desperately.

"Run," he whispered to the boy, and to hide him he spread his arms wide. "Run!" he cried.

The boy turned and ran.

What do they want? Why don't they stop? the hunchback wondered as he saw them only a few feet away, their weapons raised. He no longer understood what was happening, what their words meant, what it was they wanted.

"He let the boy get away!"

"He fooled us!"

"He's the thief!"

He wanted to ask them something, but the

first blows struck him and he fell to his knees. What did I do? he thought dazedly as a warmth spread over his face. I must tell them I love them. They are my friends. They followed me!

But there was no one there who wanted to listen to him.

chapter sixteen

Something was wrong with all of them. They were maimed, in all the evil ways that poverty and lack of hope can ruin people.

Their tempers had been sharpened to a razor-thin edge. The gray dust, carried by the autumn wind, entered their nostrils, and the chalkiness of it made their mouths dry. They resented being led by a cripple. By the time they crossed the rocky hills, they were tired, and convinced that the hunchback did not know where he was taking them, or why. But they followed him because no one had yet turned back.

The sight of the sleeping boy enraged them and they were further angered by the hunchback's gesture that told them to stop and wait. He had presumed too much. They had followed him mindlessly and listened to him for too long. His crooked back was an ugly reminder of the ugliness in their lives, and the García boy reminded them of the deaf-and-dumb girl who had run away with their future.

A current of fury went through them when the hunchback told the boy to run. His outstretched arms denied them their right to vent a rage they could no longer hold back. The rage was against their very lives, against the trap of never-changing days, as much as it was against the hunchback and his treachery. When they raised their hands against him, it was as if they had taken up arms against evil, sin, and death.

A child cried out in a wild, frightened scream and, in the sudden silence, it seemed as if the sound had come from somewhere deep within each of them. When they saw themselves reflected in each other's eyes, their faces went blank, white, and scared. They lowered their eyes to the blood-splattered rock and the motionless figure at their feet.

"What have we done?"

The question was barely audible, yet it rang like thunder and seemed to reverberate endlessly in the hollows of their hearts.

When words came, they were like drops of rain after a long drought.

"We must get him to a doctor."

"He will be all right."

"The foreigner has a car."

"He will be in Córdoba in two hours."

"Wrap his head."

"Give me your shirt; mine is dirty."

"Easy now. He just fainted."

"God have mercy on us! He is dead!"

"NO!"

They fashioned a stretcher from the shawls of the older women and carried the hunchback gently down the hill, along the path, toward the village. No one spoke. Some of the people cried. Those who carried him kept wondering why he was so light; he did not weigh more than a child.

On that long, slow walk, each of them was alone with his thoughts and yet their thoughts were alike. They had killed a man. The immensity of this fact would forever darken their lives. What kind of light could ever take that darkness away? they silently asked. And not one of them knew the answer.

chapter seventeen

When Carmen went into the house, she had wanted to gather up the things the women had given to the girl and throw them back in their faces. But when she reached the kitchen, she was overcome by a terrible helplessness, and she sat down on a chair and covered her face with her hands.

It had been an incredibly confusing morning. When she found out that the girl's bed had not been slept in, an unreasonable panic had seized her. She had rushed to tell the priest of the girl's disappearance, but when she reached his door, she had stopped. Why did she care about what happened to the girl? The girl meant nothing to her.

So she had gone about her early morning chores, trying to think of other things, of her dead son, of what she would cook for lunch and dinner, of what she would do with herself when she grew too old to work. But her thoughts kept coming back to the girl.

She thought of accidents, dangers, disasters that could have befallen the girl. Powerless to stop her thoughts, she banged pots and pans to fight off the terrible silence, the great emptiness of the house, and she grew steadily angrier with herself. But not even her anger could subdue her awareness of the girl's absence and her worries about the girl's welfare.

By the time she was ready to serve the priest's breakfast, Carmen had convinced herself that she was simply curious. Once she found out what had happened to the girl she would dismiss her from her mind. But the news that the girl had taken the statue and fled had filled her with new concerns.

On the way to get the girl's father, Carmen promised herself that she would not become involved in the girl's fate in any way. She would not speak to anyone about the statue or the girl, and she would walk away when she heard others speak of them. If she could not control her thoughts, she would at least control her acts and her tongue.

Looking at Ramón de Prada's face, unyielding

in its hardness, brought new thoughts of the girl. How had the child ever survived, Carmen wondered, so many loveless years? The hardness of her father must have been like a wall of stone. Although she neither spoke nor heard, she had eyes and her eyes, Carmen guessed, had probably never seen a tender glance nor a look of care.

Sitting at the kitchen table now, she remembered the day she had combed the girl's hair and talked of her dead son. That day she had been frightened by the understanding in the girl's eyes. And the girl had reached out with her hand, but Carmen had pushed her away.

But why should she have taken the statue? Of what possible use could the marble Child be to her? And why had she run away with it?

Maybe it was just a wish to have something of her own. Maybe the statue was to the girl what her dead son's notebook was to her. She found herself speaking one of his poems that she had always loved.

Yesterday the moon was white.
Why should it seem black to me tonight?
It is the darkness of my heart that has
Shot skyward since I rejected love.

The voices outside had grown still. In the quiet of the house, the words of the poem seemed to echo from wall to wall. Was this the answer she had been searching for?

Her heart had been too long dark from the absence of love. Perhaps she needed love as much as the girl needed to be loved. The strange thing, Carmen thought, was that she must have known this all along—from the day she first saw the girl standing in the doorway of the kitchen. But she had fought this knowledge as if she were fighting for her very life.

chapter eighteen

The priest stood by the door of the parish house until the gray dust settled on the distant path. When the last of the villagers had turned from him, disobeying and ignoring him, he knew that he had been dismissed as their priest. But far more painful than that was the realization of his failure as a human being. He who had always been merely a spectator and a judge in the war of good and evil had, for once, participated in that war. And he had lost. He expected no forgiveness for that, not even from God.

Heavily he moved across the threshold. In his study he began to write a letter to his bishop:

Throughout my life I have been guilty of the sins of pride, arrogance, and indifference.

But today I committed the gravest sin of all.
I tried to buy love I did not deserve at the
price of a human life.

He had meant to ask permission to enter a monastery so as to spend the rest of his days in solitary penance. But suddenly he felt unworthy of sanctuary within the Church. He realized that he had always had the desire to hide, to keep his distance from the realities of daily life. Had he chosen the priesthood because of this?

"Father!"

Carmen was standing next to him, and he did not want her to see that he had been crying. He blew his nose loudly and rubbed the handkerchief over his cheeks before he looked up at her and saw that her cheeks were also stained with tears.

"You must stop them from finding the girl."

How could she ask such a thing of him? Couldn't she guess that he was the weakest of men?

"You must go after them. You must stop them," she said again, her voice strong against the desperate buzzing in his head. If only she would stop telling him to do the impossible. If only she would go away.

"You must do it!"

"I could not reach them before they became a

mob," he said patiently, as if talking to a child. "I cannot stop them now."

"You must try!"

"I cannot," he said. She had put a hand on his shoulder, and he cried out to her: "Don't you see, I'm no longer their priest."

"You are my priest and the girl's," Carmen said. "What matters now is finding her. She may have gone to the forest north of here. You and the American must go there in his car. Just before the turn to the highway, you'll find a forest path. There are hunting cabins in those woods. She might be there."

"And what if she is not?" he heard himself say.

But as soon as he asked the question, he already knew the answer. Perhaps Carmen was showing him his last chance. If he could reach the girl before the villagers did, he would not be leaving in complete defeat.

"Then you will look for her until you find her," Carmen was saying. He looked up at her and smiled. She smiled back and roughly brushed the tears from her face.

"With God's help I'll find her," he said.

"And with God's help we'll make it up to her."

"We never gave her anything, did we?"

"It will be different now." Carmen's voice was very soft. "Bring her back to us."

chapter nineteen

By the time Larry Katchen reached his car, he had made a momentous decision. He would find the girl and take her with him. He would bring her to the United States, adopt her, and send her to school. He wanted badly to give her a chance at a decent future. That much he could do for her.

It would mean taking a job, teaching, lecturing, but he meant to provide her with everything he would have given to a daughter of his own. It would mean a complete change in his life, giving up the solitude to which he had grown accustomed, altering all his habits. But instead of hesitation he felt a wave of pride in himself.

The priest was coming out of the church just as Larry Katchen opened his car door.

"I want to look for the girl," Larry told him.

"Would you come with me? I wouldn't know where to start."

How swiftly God answers prayers, the priest thought, when you know what you are praying for.

They drove away from the village, down the dusty road that wound through the scarred land. Looking at this desolate landscape, Larry Katchen talked to the priest about his decision, and his reasons for it.

"It is this land that makes people the way they are—cruel and hard. They are part of the land. But the girl is not like that. I saw how gentle and soft she was with the statue. She does not belong here. I want to help her find out where she does belong, for she belongs somewhere. In a decent school, in America, she will learn what she needs to know. She will have a good life."

The priest said nothing and Larry went on, pleased with himself, happy that the terror he had seen in the hills had made him decide to protect the girl from a life among these people.

"Perhaps, when she's grown, she will decide to work with other handicapped children who need love. She has that to give. I saw her give love to Angellini's Child. I really know nothing about her, but I'm sure she has been unhappy here all her life. Almas is the wrong place for her."

"She belongs here, in our village," the priest said quietly.

Larry Katchen shook his head.

"Oh, no! It's the worst place for her."

"You are wrong. It is where she belongs."

"You have not seen your people. I saw their faces hungry for blood."

"They are famished for love," the priest said, "and you yourself said that is what the girl has to give."

"Don't you understand? Those people would kill her if she came back!"

He had shouted angrily, but the priest's face was calm, as if he had not heard.

"She belongs here," he said. "She was given to us."

Larry had wanted to spare the priest the horror he had seen in the hills. He did not want to shock this man, who obviously knew as little about people as he himself did. But in his anger he told the priest all he had witnessed and felt.

"A tragedy can alter the course of human hearts," the priest said.

"Didn't you hear me?" Larry Katchen shouted. "Those people turned into killers back in those hills! You yourself said that you did not know them. Well, I do! They're savages and the girl must be kept from them."

"If they have harmed anyone, they will not be the same ever again."

"People don't change!"

"That is not true," the priest said. "You have changed. And so have I. An act can change people, so can an idea." Larry Katchen watched the road and tried not to listen. "Sometimes we forget the most important facts," the priest continued. "I had forgotten that we did not kill Christ. If we had, we would not have survived our guilt. He died for us. That is the great difference. And it is that difference which makes me different today from the man I was yesterday."

"I don't care what you tell me about your religion," Larry said angrily. "I don't care about your people. But I do care about this young girl. I don't want her to stay among these people."

The priest said nothing. Larry thought that everything was settled now. He would find the girl, drive the priest back, pick up his things, and leave Spain with the girl, never to come back.

"The statue," he said after a while, "will be returned to your church. Your people will have what they want—what they were willing to kill for. I will take good care of the girl. She will never, never have to know what happened here. And if I were you," he turned toward the priest and spoke more gently now, "I would go away from Almas

147

too. Your God can not have anything to do with those people back there."

"My God is their God," the priest said.

They did not talk after that until they came to the forest path and began to walk. The afternoon sun sent long shafts of light through the trees onto the moss. The silence was broken only by the cracking of twigs and the rustling of dead leaves under their feet. After a while Larry Katchen turned to the priest, ashamed now of the harsh words he had spoken.

"I know," he said, "that your people are not all bad. I have seen the worst part of them—their hate. Maybe you can protect the girl against that. But she deserves a better life."

"She deserves to see hate turn into love," the priest said.

By the time they had reached the cabin, the setting sun had reddened the trees. They saw the girl sitting by the stream, the marble Child in her arms. The priest stopped Larry by placing a hand on his shoulder.

"Don't you see," he whispered, "the girl has changed both of us. She can do the same for the people of Almas. Why don't you come back with us? Why don't you stay and see it happen?"

Larry Katchen looked at the priest and smiled.

"Maybe, for a little while," he said. "To see who will be proven right."

The priest returned the smile. "Now we both seem to have faith—if not in God, then in Man."

READ YOUR WAY TO ADVENTURE

And share the joys and frustrations, triumphs and defeats of other young people.

REACH ACROSS
THE GENERATIONS

With books that explore disenchantment and discovery, failure and conquest, and seek to bridge the gap between adolescence and adulthood.

Bantam Book Catalog

Here's your up-to-the-minute listing of over 1,400 titles by your favorite authors.

This illustrated, large format catalog gives a description of each title. For your convenience, it is divided into categories in fiction and non-fiction—gothics, science fiction, westerns, mysteries, cookbooks, mysticism and occult, biographies, history, family living, health, psychology, art.

So don't delay—take advantage of this special opportunity to increase your reading pleasure.

Just send us your name and address and 50¢ (to help defray postage and handling costs).

BANTAM BOOKS, INC.
Dept. FC, 414 East Golf Road, Des Plaines, Ill. 60016

Mr./Mrs./Miss_____
(please print)

Address_____

City_____State_____Zip_____

Do you know someone who enjoys books? Just give us their names and addresses and we'll send them a catalog too!

_____

Mr./Mrs./Miss_____

Address_____

City_____State_____Zip_____

Mr./Mrs./Miss_____

Address_____

City_____State_____Zip_____

FC—9/78